LR429

Diamonds From Dr Daly

by
Angela Devine

Dales Large Print Books
Long Preston, North Yorkshire,
England.

British Library Cataloguing in Publication Data.

Devine, Angela
  Diamonds from Dr Daly.

  A catalogue record for this book is
  available from the British Library

  ISBN 1-85389-806-6 pbk

First published in Great Britain by Mills & Boon Ltd., 1992

Copyright © 1992 by Angela Devine

Cover illustration © John Heseltine by arrangement with
P.W.A. International

The moral right of the author has been asserted

Published in Large Print 1998 by arrangement with Harlequin
Books S.A.

Dales Large Print is an imprint of
Library Magna Books Ltd.
Printed and bound in Great Britain by
T.J. International Ltd., Cornwall, PL28 8RW.

CHAPTER ONE

'All I want is a life of my own, Mario! I'm twenty-six years old and a trained nurse, but I've spent my entire life in your shadow. What I want is a home of my own and a job where I'm really using my training, not just sitting around for days on end. Don't you understand?'

Sandra Calvi's blue eyes blazed with conviction as she stared imploringly at her brother. But she was wasting her time. Every line in Mario's short, powerful body radiated the energy and passion that made his concerts sell out months in advance. He gazed at her searchingly with coal-black eyes, then he erupted.

'No, I don't!' he retorted fiercely. 'Most people would give their right arm to have a job like yours. For four years you've been travelling all over the world, staying in the best hotels. London, Paris, New York, Milan, Tokyo, you've seen all of them! And you've always been well paid. But now you want to stop here in Sydney and take a job as an ordinary hospital nurse. Why? Why? Why?'

Sandra ran her fingers through her short blonde curls with an exasperated gesture.

'Because I like Sydney!' she replied. 'I grew up here.'

'No, you didn't!' contradicted Mario swiftly. 'You grew up in Italy.'

'Oh, stop scoring points!' cried Sandra impatiently. 'All right, I grew up in Italy, but I came out here when I was twelve years old, so it's the same thing. Besides, I did my training here. I still have friends here. And I've kept up my New South Wales nursing registration, so I could still get a job here!'

Mario made an angry, spluttering noise.

'A job, a job!' he echoed, snapping his fingers. 'You've already got a job, taking care of my son. What's going to become of Tony if you insist on this crazy scheme of settling in Sydney? Eh?'

'Yes, but that's part of it, Mario. Don't you see? Tony's nine years old now and he's been running wild all his life. Just because he's a haemophiliac you've spoilt him rotten. And all this travelling is ruining his school work. Lisa and I think it would be far better for Tony to stop in the one place instead of being dragged around all over the world.'

Mario's face darkened like a thundercloud passing over the sun.

'You and Lisa think what?' he demanded in a low, terrible voice.

Sandra winced, but stood her ground. 'You heard me,' she said defiantly.

Mario slammed his fist down on the occasional table, sending the glass ornaments jumping and rattling. 'Oh, yes, I heard you!' he raged. 'I wish to God I hadn't! Do you really dare to tell me that my wife and my sister are conspiring against me behind my back? Conspiring to break up my marriage and separate me from my only child? Is that what you mean, Sandra?'

Sandra rolled her eyes, wishing for the umpteenth time that Mario wouldn't be so melodramatic. Perhaps it came from all those fiery entrances and exits at the opera house. After all, the newspapers didn't call him the greatest Italian tenor in living memory for nothing.

'No, it isn't what I meant!' she replied wearily. 'I just wanted to tell you quite calmly and pleasantly that I'm thinking of getting a nursing job here in Sydney. OK?'

'OK,' agreed Mario, flashing his most charming smile. *'Va bene,* little sister. You've told me. And now I am telling-you also very calmly and pleasantly that you will do this only over my dead body!'

'Mario—' began Sandra.

'No! No, no and no! I promised Papa on his death bed that I would keep this family together. And that's what I'm going to do. You'll stay with us and take care of Tony until you marry, and that's final! And, speaking of Tony, where is he anyway?'

Sandra gave an exaggerated sigh. 'Don't panic,' she said. 'He's with Lisa. I told him to go and help set the table for lunch while I had a word with you. They're probably out on the terrace together.'

Mario snorted. Then he strode across to the window and looked out. Down below a petite, dark-haired woman was laying out cutlery on a long table, set on a terrace high above the dazzling blue waters of the harbour. She looked up and waved as Mario leaned out of the window.

'Lisa!' he called. 'Where's Tony?'

His wife brushed a stray tendril of hair out of her eyes and smiled.

'He's with Sandra,' she called back. 'Tell them to get ready if you see them. Our

8

guests will be here soon!'

Mario withdrew hastily. A look of faint uneasiness was spreading over his face.

'She says he's with you,' he explained, turning back to Sandra.

'That little brat!' breathed Sandra. 'I'll bet he's gone down to the waterfront, and if he falls on those rocks...!'

She was out of the door and running before Mario could say another word. As she raced frantically down the wide oak stairs, her heart was pumping wildly. Heaven knew, she had explained often enough to Tony how serious a simple fall could be, but the boy was as obstinate as his father—wilful, reckless and totally oblivious to danger. And ever since they had moved into this harbourside house he had spent every possible moment at the water's edge. Reaching the back door, Sandra sprinted across the brick-paved terrace, gasping an explanation to Lisa before flinging herself at the steep wooden stairs that led down the cliff-face to a small, rocky cove below. Pausing at the top of the stairs, she shaded her eyes against the glare of the sun and scanned the scene below. A speedboat was tied up at the jetty and four people had already begun the long climb up the stairs. Down on the rocks, near the water's edge, she saw two fair-haired children clambering about, but there was no sign of Tony. Then a telltale red T-shirt came into view around an outcrop of stone. Cupping her hands, Sandra shouted with all her might.

'Tony! Get off those rocks at once!'

He looked up and gave her a cheeky wave. At this distance she could not see his face, but there was an unmistakable swagger in his movements as he leapt from rock to rock. And instead of making for the stairs he was deliberately testing her out by heading along the rugged shoreline towards the other children.

'You little monkey!' cried Sandra. 'Just wait till I catch you!'

Without a second thought she went racing down the steep staircase, which zigzagged backwards and forwards down the cliff-face. She had just passed the third landing when she cannoned straight into a tall, lean man with red-gold hair who was on his way up. Strong brown hands caught her arms and steadied her.

'Whoa! Where are you off to in such a hurry?' demanded a deep, rather husky voice.

Sandra had a jumbled impression of a keen, intelligent face with a straight nose, square chin and tawny brown eyes. She tried to struggle free, but was furious to find herself imprisoned in a steely grip.

'Let me go!' she cried angrily. 'I must rescue my nephew before he hurts himself on the rocks!'

'But why all the panic?' asked her tormentor lazily. 'If you mean the little dark kid with the curly hair, he's not doing anything particularly dangerous, just climbing over the rocks with the Jessup boys. The worst he'll get from that is a bashed knee.'

'But that's exactly what I'm afraid of!' retorted Sanda. 'He's a severe haemophiliac. I don't suppose you understand, but any bleeding—'

Her companion swore softly under his breath.

'Like hell I don't!' he whipped back. 'I'm a haematologist. But don't worry, I'll catch the little brat for you.'

He was off before Sandra could even blink. Gulping for breath, she followed him. Two other strangers who were toiling up the stairs flattened themselves against the banisters at her headlong approach, but she swept by with only a gasped apology. Then, as she reached the cove, she saw that the unknown man was leaping across the rocks with all the agility of a mountain goat.

'All right, kid, hold it right there!' he shouted.

Tony turned. His curly dark hair sprang in an untidy halo around his head and his face was alight with mischief and laughter.

'Catch me!' he challenged.

And, with a rippling chuckle, he sprang towards a large, dark boulder at the water's edge. But the boulder was slimy with seaweed and disaster struck. Tony uttered a shrill cry of alarm as his feet skidded from under him.

'Tony!' cried Sandra. 'Oh, no! Are you hurt, sweetie?'

She was barely conscious of the cold rush of green sea-water among the rock pools, the slippery surface of the rocks and the strong smell of salt air as she scrambled frantically towards her nephew. Every nerve and muscle and thought was concentrated on the small, dark-haired figure who was now being scooped up in the doctor's strong arms. Not that the doctor was wasting much sympathy on him.

'You bloody little ratbag!' he roared. 'You deserve a month on bread and water for that trick. Here, let me take a took at you.'

Sandra felt an instinctive rush of annoyance at the man's brusque tone. He must have had a tough upbringing to be as harsh as that with an injured child, she thought sourly. Yet his hands were surprisingly gentle as he lifted Tony and carried him carefully back over the rocks to the jetty.

'Is he badly hurt? she demanded, crouching down beside him.

'Well, he's bleeding pretty freely, and that's not going to do him a whole lot of good. But what really worries me is that there may be bleeding into the joint. Haemarthrosis, we call it, and it can lead to crippling—'

'I know,' cut in Sandra. 'I'm a nurse.'

'Then you should have known better than to let him play on rocks like this,' he said curtly.

She bit back the outraged retort that rose to her lips and flashed the doctor a smouldering look. This was no time to argue about who was responsible for

13

Tony's accident, but resentment scorched through her like battery acid.

'Still, it's no use crying over spilt milk,' continued the stranger briskly. 'The child will need a transfusion of cryo as fast as possible to bring his Factor VIII levels up, so we'd better immobilise this leg and get him to a hospital at once. Do you have anything up at the house that we can use as splints?'

'Yes, I've got some proper medical splints,' Sandra told him through clenched teeth. 'I'll run up and get them, but in the meantime you'd better use this to try and control the bleeding.'

Rising to her feet, she lifted the hem of her dress and bit into it with strong white teeth. There was a sharp ripping sound, then she held up a length of blue and white striped cotton.

'Thanks,' replied the doctor curtly.

With deft fingers he tied the makeshift bandage tightly round Tony's injured knee. Then he glanced across at the two blond children who were hovering near the edge of the rocks and gave a shrill whistle.

'Hoy, Steve, William! Run up and tell Mrs Calvi that her son's whacked his knee and we'll have to take him to hospital.'

'Do you want them to call an ambulance?' chipped in Sandra.

'No. The Calvis have a car, don't they?' countered the stranger.

'Yes, of course.'

'Then we'll take him to the Nelson Private Hospital where I work. It's only about ten minutes' drive from here.'

The two Jessup boys were already on the terrace babbling excited explanations when Sandra came toiling up the last of the stairs. Leaving them to cope with the inevitable questions, she ran into the house and snatched up splints and bandages from the large downstairs bathroom. Then she went hurrying back down the stairs. By the time she reached the two figures at the water's edge, she could see that the unknown doctor had done everything possible to make Tony comfortable. A cushion, presumably fetched from the motorboat, was under the boy's head and his leg was stretched out with a lightweight man's jacket rolled up beneath it. Even so, Tony was biting back tears of pain.

'The leg's not fractured, is it?' asked Sandra, setting down the equipment she had brought.

'No, but the joint is getting pretty

15

swollen. Anyway, let's get him bandaged up and then we can take him to hospital and have a proper look.'

Unwinding the makeshift strip of Sandra's dress from the boy's leg, he swiftly cleaned the wound, put a splint at the back of the knee and bandaged the leg firmly.

'Right. Ready to go, mate?' he asked.

Tony's face was still screwed up tautly, but he gave the doctor a ghost of his usual cheeky smile.

'Yep,' he agreed.

'Good on you. Just put your arms around my neck and I'll carry you up as gently as I can. What's your name, sport?'

'Tony. Tony Calvi. What's yours?'

'Richard Daly,' replied the doctor.

Then, with effortless strength, he whisked the injured child up in his arms and bounded up the stairs two at a time. Even though she was not carrying a thirty-kilogram child, Sandra had trouble keeping up with him. By the time they reached the top she was breathless as well as bedraggled. An anxious Lisa came hurrying across the terrace to meet them, looking pale and shaken. Clutching Tony's dangling hand, she gazed up at Richard

16

Daly with strained dark eyes.

'Is he going to be all right?' she demanded.

'I'd say so,' he agreed in an exasperated voice. 'Although it wasn't very smart to let him go running around on those rocks. He'll need a transfusion as fast as possible, so we'd better get moving. Can I take your car?'

Lisa ran her fingers distractedly through her lustrous black hair and stared helplessly around her.

'Yes, of course. It's in the garage. But we've got a dozen more people about to arrive for lunch. What on earth am I going to do?'

Sandra stepped into the breach with the ease of long practice. Lisa's gaze was fixed apprehensively on the red strain seeping through her son's makeshift bandage and Sandra knew that tears were not far away. And Richard Daly's brusque handling of the situation certainly wouldn't help matters. Stifling her instinctive dislike of the man, Sandra forced herself to speak pleasantly.

'Go and get in the car, Lisa,' she said. 'Dr Daly, do you mind driving, since you know the way? And—Mr and Mrs Jessup, isn't it? Do please sit down and make yourselves comfortable. I'll just tell my brother what's going on and then I'll stay and deal with the lunch.'

Pausing only to see that Richard Daly was shepherding everybody into the car, she rushed into the house. With a quick sprint from the kitchen to the bathroom, she gathered up ice packs, Tony's medical card and a couple of clean towels. Then she rushed back out on to the terrace, almost colliding with Mario, who had just emerged from the living-room with a tray of drinks. A great torrent of Italian ensued as explanations and questions flew back and forth. Once assured that his son was unlikely to die, Mario insisted on staying to look after his guests and sent Sandra hurrying towards the car with a gentle push.

'Go on, *cara*. Go with them, I beg you,' he urged. 'You know how Tony relies on you. We all do. And Lisa will go to pieces if you aren't there while they treat him. You know how she hates hospitals.'

You cunning, manipulative beast! thought Sandra admiringly. She knew perfectly well that her brother was using this opportunity to show her how indispensable her nursing skills were. And yet she was still fond of him, and much of what he was saying was true. Lisa would go to pieces without her. So she pecked Mario hastily on the cheek and surrendered.

'All right,' she grumbled. 'But I know what you're up to, Mario! And I won't give in to blackmail!'

He gave her the full melting charm of his heart-warming smile and pinched her cheek.

'Go on,' he urged, pushing her into the back seat of the car.

Richard Daly was already seated behind the steering-wheel and Tony was lying on the back seat, with his leg elevated on a pile of cushions hastily snatched from the lounge furniture on the terrace. Lisa was sitting in the front passenger seat, which might have surprised anyone who didn't know her well. But it only made Sandra give a resigned sigh. Her sister-in-law was deathly pale and was keeping her eyes carefully turned away from the sight of her son's bleeding leg. With her left hand she held a crumpled handkerchief pressed to her mouth. Her right arm was stretched uncomfortably over the back of the seat so that she could hold Tony's hand.

19

Sandra slipped cautiously into place, and set the ice packs and towels around the child's knee.

'Just move your hand, Lisa,' she requested. 'I want to make sure his leg is comfortable.'

'My poor little Tony!' said Lisa with a tremor in her voice.

Glancing up, Sandra met Richard Daly's gaze in the rear-view mirror and saw the swift flicker of impatience in his eyes. She felt a surge of pure rage flow through her. How dared he make judgements about Lisa like that? Although Sandra had often been exasperated by Lisa's squeamishness herself, she found that it was quite another matter to see a stranger reacting to it. You pig, she thought, as the car puffed up the driveway and into the road. You arrogant, callous, insensitive pig! I hope this is the last time I ever have anything to do with you!

All the casual holiday atmosphere of weekend Sydney flashed past them. First the lavish mansions on the waterfront with their immaculate gardens and panoramic views. Then a shopping centre, deserted except for lovers wandering arm in arm in casual beach clothes and children dawdling along, licking ice-creams. After that came an older section of the city where red terraced houses were jumbled together in rows with frangipani bushes and dark blue convolvulus spilling over the walls on their tiny front gardens. At last they turned into a driveway in a seaside suburb and the car came to a halt outside a large apricot brick building with a huge red 'CASUALTY' sign hanging above a concrete ambulance bay.

Richard Daly disappeared inside the building and returned with a trolley. Lifting Tony out of the car, he laid him flat and buckled a strap around him to prevent him from falling. With an unexpectedly gentle touch he smoothed the boy's tangled curls back from his forehead and winked at him.

'Don't worry, mate,' he said soothingly. 'We'll have you fixed up in no time.'

The casualty ward was a large L-shaped room with cubicles opening all the way down one side. In the other wing of the L were filing cabinets, office space, a door leading to a waiting-room for patients with minor injuries. Sandra glanced around her, feeling instantly at home amid the oxygen cylinders, defibrillating equipment, metal

21

trolleys and I/V lines. But the place was obviously having quite the reverse effect on Lisa, who paled visibly as Tony was wheeled into the assessment-room.

'I'll need to get some medical details about Tony, please, Mrs Calvi,' said Richard briskly. 'Everything you can tell me about his history, his blood type, his Factor VIII levels, how much cryo he normally requires in these situations, what previous treatment he's had, et cetera. I assume you've brought his medical card with you?'

Lisa flinched.

'I can never remember all that stuff,' she muttered despairingly. 'It makes my head spin.'

Richard sighed impatiently.

'Perhaps you could think about it while I go and get an admission form,' he suggested.

'Sandra—' began Lisa imploringly.

'Don't worry, Lisa,' said Sandra. 'I'll handle it.'

She followed Richard out to the administrative area in the other wing of the ward.

'Do you have to be so prickly with her?' she demanded, as he came to a halt in front of a filing cabinet.

'Mrs Calvi doesn't seem to understand that her son could bleed to death from an episode like this,' he said in a taut undertone.

'She understands!' snapped Sandra. 'That's exactly why she's going to pieces. Lisa's the kind of person who finds it hard to cope with the sight of blood, let alone the risk of death.'

Richard smiled grimly.

'Not an ideal qualification for the mother of a haemophiliac,' he remarked.

'No—well, it's not the kind of job people fall over themselves applying for, is it?' flashed Sandra. 'Lisa's doing the best she can in a very difficult situation. But it might help if you would show her some compassion.'

He snorted. 'It might help even more if she could produce this child's medical records,' he retorted. 'As it is, I suppose I'd better take a blood sample to determine his blood group and go on from there.'

'That won't be necessary,' she snapped, producing the plastic wallet that contained Tony's medical data. 'His blood type is O-positive, he's a severe haemophiliac with less than one per cent Factor VIII in his blood and he's had several previous haemarthroses in Sydney, all of which were treated at the Montgomery Hospital. You'll find details of the amounts of cryo which were used on the card. A complete coagulation evaluation of the entire family was done when his condition was first diagnosed and no history of haemophilia was discovered. We can only assume that some mutation in the X chromosome was responsible for it.'

'That's more than likely,' muttered Richard. 'Twenty-five per cent of the new cases we see each year fall into that category.'

'I know,' agreed Sandra crisply. 'And if there's anything else you want to know about Tony's illness just ask me.'

'All right,' agreed Richard grudgingly. 'But where do you come into all this anyway?'

'My name is Sandra Calvi,' she said crisply. 'I'm Tony's aunt. I'm also employed as a private nurse to look after him.'

'Hmm!' he snorted. 'It's a pity you don't do a better job of it. Letting him run around on rocks like that was totally irresponsible.'

She took a deep breath and counted to ten before she trusted herself to answer. 'Tony wasn't actually on the rocks with my permission,' she pointed out sweetly.

'Well, whether he was or not, we'll still have to fix up the damage, won't we?' he countered. 'Now, if you'll just go back and sit with him for a while, I'll send a clerk along to get the admission details.'

Sandra walked away seething. But however much she disliked Richard Daly she had to admit he was efficient. Within a short time Tony had been moved from the assessment-room into a cubicle and details had been taken down by a clerk. After that the casualty doctor on duty came in, accompanied by Richard Daly, who had changed into clean clothes and a white lab coat. Once the doctor on duty had taken a history and examined the boy, Richard sat comfortably in a chair and looked at Lisa. When he spoke his tone was no longer quite so brusque.

'I'll just have to do some basic investigations now, Mrs Calvi,' he explained. 'A blood count, clotting studies, that sort of thing. I'll have to take a blood sample from Tony's arm, but that shouldn't cause him too much discomfort. We also want to do an X-ray, just to exclude the possibility of a fracture. After that, when all the results are back, I think it would be a good idea if I take him into Theatre and aspirate the blood from the joint.'

'Aspirate...?' she queried.

Lisa looked fearfully at Sandra. But it was Richard who replied.

'It's nothing to worry about,' he said soothingly. 'As you can see, the joint is very stiff and swollen because of all the internal bleeding. All I want to do is take Tony into Theatre, where the conditions are sterile, and take that blood out of his knee with a needle. He'll feel much more comfortable when it's done.'

Before long treatment was in full swing. To the Calvis' relief an X-ray ruled out the possibility of a fracture, although the blood count and clotting studies confirmed that Tony needed a hefty transfusion of Factor VIII. Once he received the missing factor, which would allow his blood to clot, Sandra knew that his recovery would be rapid. She also noticed approvingly that Dr Daly gave orders for the pain-killer to be given through the drip rather than by injection. This method would avoid causing any additional pain to the boy.

Lisa too seemed very happy with the standard of care at the Nelson Hospital. When Tony was finally brought back from Theatre and Richard came to reassure them that he was doing well Lisa flung herself impetuously at him and kissed him on both cheeks.

'Thank you, Dr Daly,' she cried emotionally. 'You've been wonderful!'

Richard looked rather taken aback.

'Well, it was a lucky coincidence that you invited a haematologist to lunch,' he said with a shrug.

'Coincidence—tch!' replied Lisa scornfully. 'I'm sorry, Dr Daly. I must admit that it wasn't only because you're Wendy Jessup's neighbour that I asked you to come. Wendy's been telling me for weeks what a brilliant doctor you are, and I thought if you came to lunch you might persuade my husband to see sense about Tony.'

'In what way?' asked Richard with a puzzled frown.

'About all the travelling we do with the boy. I'm sure it's not good for Tony to be dragged around on these overseas trips, but Mario won't listen to me, or Sandra. I thought he might take notice of you, if I

27

could steer the conversation round to it.'

For the first time Sandra heard Richard Daly laugh—a low, throaty chuckle that was oddly contagious.

'You're a very devious woman, Mrs Calvi,' he said reprovingly. 'But I must say I think you're right. It certainly isn't ideal for a severe haemophiliac like Tony to be constantly on the move. And I'd be happy to talk to Mr Calvi on the subject whenever you like to arrange it.'

Lisa smiled radiantly at him.

'Thank you,' she beamed. 'Now, when can I see my little Tony?'

'Whenever you like,' replied Richard. 'He's been transferred to the children's ward and I'd like to keep him in for a day or two just to make sure his Factor VIII levels are back where they should be. But you're welcome to go up and visit him. It's on the third floor just along from the lifts.'

'Thank you!' exclaimed Lisa again. 'And you too, Sandra. Tell Mario not to expect me for a few hours!'

And, with a brief wave, she vanished down the corridor.

'Lisa!' called Sandra in exasperation, rushing after her. 'Come back! I haven't got any money or keys!'

But when she reached the lift the doors had already closed.

'Damn!' she said with feeling, and pressed the 'UP' button. 'Now I'll have to chase after her!'

'Don't do that,' ordered a husky voice. 'I'll get you safely home.'

CHAPTER TWO

Sandra swung round and saw Richard Daly looming above her with an amused expression on his face. She let out a sigh of pure annoyance.

'There's no need!' she snapped. 'I can manage.'

'I'm sure you can,' he agreed serenely. 'But why bother your sister-in-law when she's just been through a very stressful afternoon? We can take a taxi to my place and then I'll get my car and drive you home. Or are you too much of a wimp to go off alone with a big bad stranger?'

Sandra hesitated, stung by the mockery in his voice. The last thing she wanted

29

was to accept a ride from Richard Daly, but she didn't want him thinking she was frightened of him either.

'No, I'm not,' she said coolly. 'Thank you, Dr Daly, I'd be very grateful if you'd take me home.'

Richard must have had spare clothes at the hospital, for he was now wearing a crisp brown and white shirt, brown corduroy trousers and a beige jacket. In her torn dress, soaked with blood and sea-water, Sandra could not help feeling at a disadvantage. She was already smarting from his snide comments about her care of Tony, and it seemed doubly humiliating to look so bedraggled. The sooner this is over, the better, she thought with annoyance as the taxi sped through the suburbs.

Ten minutes later they were climbing out of the vehicle in a leafy harbourside suburb not far from her own home. Richard opened an ornate black iron gate and led Sandra through on to a sandstone path which wound out of sight between lush pink hibiscus bushes.

'The house is down by the water's edge,' he explained. 'You can't see it until you're practically on top of it.'

Sandra paused and bent forward to sniff

a strongly scented frangipani flower. Then her fingers travelled up to touch the waxy perfection of its yellow and white petals. She loved gardens, but it was a taste not shared by her brother. In spite of Mario's wealth most of the last four years had been spent in luxurious city hotels with little trace of greenery.

'What a beautiful place!' she said with feeling. 'Do you do your own gardening?'

Richard looked appalled. 'Good God, no!' he replied. 'I'm hardly ever home. I have a gardener who comes in, and he's very keen. His latest project is refinishing all the sandstone paths. By the way, you'd better watch your step along here. It's a bit uneven.'

His warning came just a fraction too late, as Sandra's foot caught in a crevice and she gave a low gasp of surprise. But Richard's reflexes were swift. He caught her instantly by the arm and steadied her.

'Thank you,' she murmured.

To her surprise his warm grip on her arm seemed to be sending odd flutters of excitement through her body. It was an unnerving experience and, with an uncertain smile, she moved away.

'I'll be fine now,' she assured him.

The path descended steeply through flowering shrubs and a grotto surrounded by ferns to a point where the roof of a house suddenly materialised at their feet. Sandra stared down at the orange tiles in surprise.

'It does seem to spring out at you, doesn't it?' she remarked.

'That's one of the reasons why I bought the place,' agreed Richard. 'I liked the way the house blended in with the environment. But it's not a log cabin, by any means. Come and take a took.'

He led her down a flight of sandstone stairs which opened out on to a huge patio with a jade-green swimming-pool gleaming invitingly in its centre. Sandra stepped hesitantly forward and tilted her head to look at the house.

'It's absolutely gorgeous!' she said delightedly. 'It's just like the villas back home in Italy.'

In fact the house was built in a completely authentic Mediterranean style. It was two storeys high with all the features Sandra remembered from her childhood in Italy—walls covered in mellow gold stucco, green wooden shutters at the windows, terracotta orange roof tiles and an arched

32

loggia providing shade along the ground floor. Even the plants on the terrace looked distinctively Mediterranean. A tall, slender cypress tree grew in an angle next to the house, bright red geraniums cascaded from classical urns and a purple wistaria hung gracefully from a trellis. I'd love to have a home like this, thought Sandra enviously.

'That's the garage right there,' said Richard, gesturing at another stucco-covered building to one side of the terrace. 'But if you don't mind I'll just dash inside and make a quick phone call about a patient before I drive you home.'

'Of course,' she agreed warily. 'Shall I wait in the car?'

Richard's golden-brown eyes suddenly met hers in an amused glance.

'I'm not actually going to seduce you if you set foot inside the house,' he assured her mockingly.

Sandra flushed. 'I didn't think you were,' she retorted hastily.

'Good. So why don't you come in and make yourself comfortable? In fact, you might as well have a quick shower and put some clean clothes on while you're at it.'

'Oh, that won't be necessary,' she said in alarm.

'Yes, it will,' he replied lazily. 'Then you won't get my car so dirty when I drive you home.'

Put that way, his suggestion seemed unanswerable. With a feeling of mounting uneasiness, Sandra followed him into the arched loggia that led to the front door. He produced a key and opened the door, then ushered her into a hall with a finely patterned mosaic floor. She followed him up the oak staircase and looked curiously about her. With a thoughtful frown Richard flung open a door, revealing a large bedroom dominated by a huge half-tester bed hung with green draperies. The room was beautifully furnished with a bow-fronted mahogany chest of drawers, a carved French wardrobe and a couch upholstered in gold velvet. However, the effect was spoilt slightly by a wet-suit flung carelessly on the couch and a pile of power-boat magazines and medical journals leaning drunkenly on the bedside table. But Richard seemed oblivious to this clutter. He stood still in front of the chest of drawers, scratching his head.

'Now the problem is to find you something to wear,' he muttered. 'I don't think I've got anything suitable to offer you, unless you're willing to swim in one of my tracksuits.'

'Anything would be better than what I'm swimming in at the moment,' replied Sandra ruefully, looking down at the blood and sea-water on her ruined dress.

Richard's lips curved. His smile was slightly crooked and had a mischievous charm that made him seem far more approachable.

'I suppose you're right,' he admitted. 'Well, take these, then.'

He hauled a pair of dark blue nylon tracksuit trousers and a matching wind-cheater out of a drawer and passed them to her.

'Now, come and I'll get you a towel,' he invited. 'There's a spare bedroom next door with its own bathroom. You can use that. Take your time and just come downstairs when you're ready.'

The spare bedroom proved to be another pleasant, sunny room with French windows and a balcony overlooking the harbour. It was decorated in pale blue and white, and the same colours were repeated in the adjoining bathroom. Stepping under the warm downpour of the shower, Sandra closed her eyes and exhaled blissfully. The drama with Tony, coming straight on the heels of her quarrel with Mario, had left her feeling like a washed-out rag, and it was wonderful to relax and stop thinking. Yet, when she finally turned off the shower and groped for a large, fluffy bathtowel, there was still a faint, worried frown on her face. She felt slightly dazed by finding herself in the home of a complete stranger, and it didn't help that her feelings towards Richard Daly were so confused.

At first she had disliked him instinctively, resenting his abrasive, dictatorial manner and the way he seemed to blame her for Tony's accident. But fairness forced her to admit that he was an excellent doctor, even if he did run over people like a human steamroller. Anyway, it wasn't as if she would have to see him again after today. All she had to do was get a ride home with him and that would be the end of it. With that thought, she began hastily pulling on the clothes that Richard had lent her. His tracksuit was far too long for her, so that she had to roll up the sleeves and the ankles. As she came down the stairs she picked her way carefully to avoid tripping over the furled material.

'Oh, there you are,' said Richard, coming

out of the kitchen with a glass of beer in one hand and a large hunk of French bread slathered in pâté in the other. 'Sorry about this. I know it's extremely rude of me, but I suddenly realised I was starving.'

'I don't blame you,' replied Sandra with feeling. 'It's after three o'clock. I'm starving myself.'

'Well, look, I'll tell you what,' he suggested. 'Why don't you stay and have a bite to eat here? With all the uproar at your place today, they've probably either given up on lunch or finished it ages ago. I can't offer you anything very fancy, but there's plenty of ham and salad.'

She gave him a disconcerted look. An intimate lunch with somebody she knew well was one thing, but with a total stranger? Especially a stranger who had been so critical of her nursing skills?

'I don't think—' she began.

But Richard cut in. As if he had read her mind, he gave her his engagingly lopsided smile. 'Look, I think you and I got off on the wrong foot today,' he said frankly. 'And I'm sorry about it. I didn't mean to imply that you were negligent with Tony. But if you stay on and have lunch with me we can

37

discuss the best way of tackling the boy's problems.'

Sandra gave him a suspicious glance.

'I think I'm being conned,' she protested.

He grinned wickedly.

'Yes, you are,' he agreed. 'But I can't help being intrigued by what's going on in the Calvi household. Besides, I'd genuinely like you to stay. And I promise not to interrogate you until you've had your meal.'

She felt a strange breathlessness overtake her, as if she had been running too fast. And with it came a piercing realisation that she wanted to stay. Not only for the chance of eating some of that deliciously crusty bread, but also to find out more about this odd man, who was beginning to fascinate her.

'All right,' she agreed.

Richard was as good as his word. It was not until they had both demolished large plates of honey-cured ham, crisp lettuce and tomato and hunks of bread and pâté that he returned to the subject of her quarrel with Mario. By then they were at a table overlooking the harbour, and Sandra sat gazing out at the passing yachts with a half-empty glass of Sauternes resting idly in her hand. She couldn't help thinking that the sweet, pale gold wine must be stronger than it looked, for a giddy, bubbling sensation was spreading all through her. In this dreamy state Richard's question caught her off guard. Setting down a platter of cheese and fruit, he looked at her shrewdly.

'So what's big brother Mario black-mailing you to do?' he demanded.

Sandra caught her breath and gave a wry gasp of laughter.

'What do you mean?' she parried.

'I couldn't help overhearing your wonderfully intriguing line as we were getting into the car,' he explained. 'And I'm an expert at dragging information out of people, so you might as well tell me what's going on. I don't much like the thought of that kid being at the centre of some kind of family tug-of-war.'

Sandra took another sip of the wine and stared moodily out at the busy harbour. Normally she would not have dreamt of confiding in a stranger, but tension had been building up in her for months over this issue. And there was something about Richard's expression that was totally implacable.

'Oh, all right,' she grumbled. 'But it's rather long and complicated.'

Haltingly she told him of the years she had spent as a private nurse to her haemophiliac nephew. Dazzling years, full of glamour and international travel, and yet oddly frustrating too.

'The trouble is,' she finished, 'that Mario has never really accepted the seriousness of Tony's condition. Oh, he pays me to nurse him, but he doesn't honestly seem to believe that anything much is wrong with the child. Poor little Tony's been dragged from pillar to post for years, but now that he's getting older it's harder and harder to supervise him adequately. I can't help feeling that there's a disaster just waiting to happen.'

'So what would you like to do about it?' demanded Richard.

'I'd like Lisa and Tony to settle in Sydney and make a home here while Mario goes on tour alone,' said Sandra.

'That's obviously the best thing for the child,' replied Richard. 'But that wasn't what I meant. What about you? What do you want out of life?'

Sandra sighed. 'Well, I originally trained as a nurse precisely because I wanted to help with Tony,' she explained. 'But as time passed I realised I wanted to do nursing for its own sake. What I'd really like more than anything else is a job in a hospital, but Mario won't hear of it. He says it will break up the family.'

Richard snorted sceptically.

'If you've been a qualified nurse for five years, you must be at least in your mid-twenties, aren't you?' he demanded.

'Yes,' she agreed with a sigh. 'I'm twenty-six.'

'Then in that case, sweetheart, I'd say it was high time the family was broken up. Don't you find it completely suffocating to live with your brother and his family when you're a grown woman?'

Sandra smiled wryly. 'Yes,' she admitted. 'I can't even go out on a date without having Mario hanging around to clock me back in at midnight. And if I see the same chap more than twice he wants to know whether I'm planning to get married. It infuriates me so much that there are times when I want to do something totally outrageous.'

Richard gave a throaty chuckle.

'Well,' he said briskly, 'finish your lunch and then we'll put our heads together. If we really try hard, I'm sure we can think of something totally outrageous for you to do.'

'Whatever do you mean?' she asked nervously.

'Let's see,' he said, popping a grape into his mouth and chewing thoughtfully. 'You've made a good beginning, having lunch with a total stranger. Why don't we follow it up with a spin on the harbour in my speedboat and then dinner and a nightclub? And, if you promise not to turn into a pumpkin at midnight, I won't take you home until two a.m. What do you say?'

Sandra could say nothing for a moment. Yet her eyes twinkled mischievously.

'Wouldn't it be fun?' she murmured. 'But Mario would have a fit!'

Richard grinned back at her with a challenging glint in his tawny eyes.

'Speaking as a medical man,' he remarked wickedly, 'I'd say it would do Mario all the good in the world to have a fit.'

She choked with laughter. 'Oh, it's quite impossible,' she said regretfully. 'Besides, how could I go out to dinner and a nightclub dressed in your old tracksuit?'

Richard's eyes narrowed. 'That is a

bit of a problem,' he admitted. 'Going home first would spoil the fun, wouldn't it? And of course Mario would probably demand three signed character witnesses before he'd let you out with me. There must be some way round it, though.'

He thought for a moment, then snapped his fingers.

'Got it!' he exclaimed. 'Wendy Jessup!'

Sandra looked blank.

'My next-door neighbour,' he explained. 'Don't you remember? The Jessups were the people who brought me along to the lunch at your place. They're probably home again by now, and Wendy's a really good sort. She's about your size, too. I'll bet she'd lend you some clothes if I explained it all to her.'

Sandra would sooner have walked over hot coals than made such a request, but Richard seemed to have enough nerve for anything. He vanished next door and was soon back with a selection of evening dresses draped over one arm and a bag full of accessories dangling from the other.

'Wendy thinks it's a great idea,' he said casually. 'Lisa's told her all about the plot to stay in Sydney and she agrees that you should cut the apron-strings. She's also agreed to phone Mario about nine o'clock and tell him that you're out with me and won't be home till late. So I think I've got everything under control.'

You certainly have, thought Sandra an hour or so later as they skimmed swiftly over the dark blue waters of the harbour. Richard was holding the wheel of the speedboat with a relaxed, easy confidence, but his face was alight with exhilaration as he sent the craft hurtling along amid clouds of spray. Somehow his exuberance was infectious, and Sandra had the heady, breathless feeling that she was on a runaway roller-coaster. Her initial antagonism to Richard still hadn't completely died down and she suspected that he could be quite harsh and ruthless if he were crossed. Yet he also had tremendous charm and vitality.

There ought to be danger signs put up around a man like that, she thought. Even though he seems so suave, he's absolutely unstoppable once he wants something. Irresistible, you might say. And in more ways than one. Richard's powerful physique and rugged features exercised a magnetism that no woman could ignore. Sandra only had to look at him to feel a thrill of excitement coursing through her veins, along with an unnerving desire to reach out and touch him. Sensing her gaze, he glanced across and winked at her.

'Having fun?' he asked.

'Yes,' she replied swiftly.

Too swiftly. When he turned his gaze back to the water a brief frown replaced Sandra's smile. Even though she was loving every minute of this escapade she had an ominous feeling that there would be hell to pay when it was over. Uncannily Richard seemed to know exactly what she was thinking. Taking one hand off the wheel, he reached out to squeeze her arm.

'Stop worrying about Mario and enjoy yourself!' he said severely. 'That's an order.'

It was an order she found increasingly easy to obey as the evening sped by. The spin on the harbour was followed by a quick change and dinner in a restaurant with a wonderful view of the city lights. Dressed in a black suit with a crisp white shirt, and viewed through a haze of candle-light, Richard looked more irresistible than ever. And the background melodies of Chopin sonatas from a grand piano and the tinkle of glass and silver didn't help matters either. By the time she had finished her seafood avocado and embarked on a juicy tournedos with mushrooms Sandra was well aware that she was losing her head over Dr Daly. But she was too reckless to resist. Nothing like this had ever happened to her before. All her life she had been the quiet, calm, sensible sort of person who everybody relied on in emergencies, and she was sick of it. Just for once she wanted to let herself go with the kind of fire and passion and instinctive sense of abandon that people like Mario and Lisa always showed.

So when Richard smiled warmly at her in the haze of candle-light she smiled back with all her heart. And when he drew her against him on the dance-floor and held her close, with his cheek resting on her soft, fair curls, she let herself sway sinuously against him. And when he finally brought her home, sparkling with pleasure and chattering brightly at two in the morning, she did something that was even more unlike her. She let him kiss her with a passion that shocked and enthralled her.

The house and patio were bathed in silvery moonlight as he stopped his car on

46

the roadside and came to open her door. Taking her hand, he led her down the path, and she breathed in deeply, enjoying the cool, scented night air and the feeling of his warm hand engulfing hers. At the foot of the path he came to a halt and touched her cheek lightly.

'Thanks for a wonderful evening,' he said.

Her hand came up and covered his fingers. 'I'm the one who should be thanking you,' she replied. 'It's been absolutely magical!'

And, standing on her toes, she kissed him impulsively on the cheek. What followed astonished her, for she found herself suddenly caught hard against his body so that she could feel the violent thudding of his heart through his jacket. Then his questing fingers tilted her chin and his mouth came down on hers. Sandra couldn't claim never to have been kissed, but she had certainly never been kissed like that before. Desire spiralled dizzily through her as Richard's warm lips met hers and his tongue took fierce possession of her mouth. Instinctively she arched her back and pressed herself against him, giving back all the warmth and passion that he was rousing in her. He broke away with a gasp, then nuzzled her neck, sending shivers of excitement through her. Then he released her and stepped back with a complete change of manner.

'Listen,' he said briskly. 'Are you serious about wanting a job in a hospital?'

Disappointment flooded through her. Obviously that kiss was nothing more than a moment's idle flirtation to Richard Daly. Well, she wasn't going to let, him see how much that hurt her!

'Yes,' she replied in an offhand tone.

'Good. Well, we're desperately short of nurses at the Nelson Hospital where I work, so I'll arrange an interview for you tomorrow morning with one of the assistant directors of nursing. She'll probably want you to start work on Tuesday or Wednesday.'

Sandra's mouth fell open.

'B-but I can't!' she stammered. 'Mario won't—'

'Mario won't have any say in the matter,' cut in Richard firmly. 'What's more, I'll pick you up myself at nine o'clock tomorrow to make sure you don't get cold feet and back out. I'll see you then.'

And, with a casual wave of the hand, he went bounding up the path, leaving Sandra totally aghast, wondering what on earth she had let herself in for.

CHAPTER THREE

Chinks of sunlight were already creeping round the edges of the window when Sandra woke the following morning. Blinking sleepily, she stumbled across and drew back the curtains. A flood of light poured in. Although it was only a little after seven o'clock it promised to be a perfect day. The air was already mild and warm with a strong scent of salt and a lesser undertone of tropical flowers. Leaning out of the window, Sandra gazed appreciatively at the harbour. With its dazzling blue expanse broken by the white foaming wake of the early morning ferries, it looked like a newly finished oil painting. Humming softly to herself, she withdrew into the bedroom and ambled away to take her shower.

Yet all the time that she was shampooing

her hair and towelling herself dry her mind was filled with a single thought: Richard Daly. Wrapping a towel around her like a sarong, she padded back into the bedroom and took a hairdrier out of the bottom drawer of her dressing-table. As she unwound the flex she glimpsed herself in the mirror. To her annoyance she saw that she looked like a starry-eyed teenager. Her blue eyes were wistful and there was a dreamy half-smile lurking around the corners of her mouth.

You fool, Sandra! she told herself severely. You're supposed to be the calm, sensible one of this family. It's ridiculous to go mooning around like a lovesick fifteen-year-old just because some chap kissed you. It doesn't mean a thing! And anyway, how much do you even know about Richard Daly?

Precious little, she had to admit, as she plugged in the drier and almost deafened herself with the resulting noise. Except that he was calm and competent at dealing with Tony, but you'd expect that from a professional. And he didn't waste much sympathy on him, did he? Her lips curved into a reminiscent smile as she remembered Richard's exasperated comments. All the same, his hands had been very gentle as he held the injured child. And, even though his sarcastic comments had wounded her deeply, she had been impressed by his obvious efficiency at his job.

All right, so he's competent, she admitted. But what else do you know about him? Only that he rolls right over people when he wants something, but he has so much charm that nobody seems to mind. Apart from that it's all external stuff. His clothes are casual, but very stylish, he owns a beautiful and obviously expensive house, he's in his mid to late thirties and is good-looking in a rugged sort of way. And being kissed by him is rather like being swept off your feet by gale-force winds...

She paused in the act of feathering a handful of curls under the blast of the drier and pulled a face.

You're at it again, Sandra! she told herself exasperatedly. Anyone would think you were madly in love with the man.

With a quickening heartbeat, she wondered whether she was. Her thoughts strayed back to the one and only time she had ever come close to getting married. Ken Jablonski had been a surgeon at a leading New York hospital. He was stable,

51

sensible, reliable, all the things that Sandra had always admired. And anxious to marry her into the bargain. She was fond of Ken, and yet some vital spark had always seemed to be missing between them. It was her sister-in-law Lisa, with her eagle eye, who had noticed the growing heaviness in Sandra's step, her long, pensive silences as Ken's proposals grew more pressing. And it was Lisa's impassioned advice that had finally made Sandra draw back from the brink. *'Aspetta il fulmine!'* Lisa had cried, waving her arms around. 'Wait for the thunderbolt, Sandra! Don't marry without love! You'll regret it.'

Over the last two years, as her dissatisfaction with her lifestyle grew, Sandra had often wondered whether she had been crazy to listen to Lisa. Yet now she was beginning to suspect that Lisa might be right. Her lips twitched as she remembered that thrilling speedboat ride with Richard Daly and the feeling of exhilaration that had swept through her. Perhaps people really could be struck by a thunderbolt and fall instantly, madly in love. Or then again, perhaps it was all nonsense.

'Either way,' she said severely to her reflection, 'if you don't hurry up and get dressed, you won't even be ready when he comes to get you.'

She hesitated over her choice of clothes for the job interview, but finally chose a lightweight suit with pale blue and cream stripes, which she had bought in Milan during the European summer. It was superbly cut and managed to look both casual and dressy, while the blue brought out the colour of her eyes. A quick dusting of blusher high on her cheekbones, a touch of grey eye-shadow around her eyes and some glossy coral lipstick made her feel ready to face the world. After a moment's hesitation she sprayed a light mist of Chanel No 5 on her wrists and throat.

As she picked her way slowly down the staircase her stomach was churning with nerves. Three ordeals in one morning, she thought. Breaking the news to Mario, seeing Richard again and being interviewed for the job. But the worst one of all will be tackling Mario. Just as well he didn't see me kissing Richard last night or the fat would really be in the fire!

The fragrance of freshly brewed coffee led her out on to the terrace, where Lisa and Mario were sitting at a table set with a fine lace tablecloth and exquisite bone china. In the centre of the table were two large baskets, one containing assorted pastries, the other fresh fruit. There was also a crystal jug of freshly squeezed orange juice. Sandra sat down in her usual place and Lisa flashed her a swift, nervous smile.

'Good morning,' said Sandra brightly, feeling like a character on stage.

Mario slowly folded up his copy of *Opera Australia* and gazed at her piercingly from beneath dark, over-hanging brows.

'What were you doing kissing that bastard of a doctor on the front path in the middle of the night?' he demanded without preamble.

'Mario!' protested Lisa. She laid her hand pleadingly on her husband's arm, but he shook it off and stared fiercely at Sandra.

'Eh? Answer me!' he roared.

'Mind your own business!' flared Sandra.

It was not a promising beginning. With shaking fingers, she picked up a croissant and tore it apart. She went on grimly buttering it and spreading it with jam while Mario ranted and raved and stormed around the patio. His voice grew louder and more vibrant till she expected him at any moment to burst into song—some aria about shame and death and a family brought to ruin by a woman's forbidden love. Lisa gave her an expressive look and passed the coffee percolator. Wincing at the increasing volume, Sandra poured herself a cup of coffee.

'And another thing!' added Mario, warming to his theme. 'Back in Orvieto, in the old days, we didn't go kissing girls in full view of their families in the middle of the night. Most of the marriages were arranged. Lots of men only ever met their brides once or twice before they were married. But does this *maledetto Australiano* come and ask me for your hand in marriage? Does he? Eh? Eh? No, he thinks he can have it all without even a word of explanation to your family.'

'Oh, Mario!' said Sandra crossly. 'Who said anything about marriage anyway?'

It was not the right response. Mario stared at her incredulously, then took a long, indignant breath. He was just launching into an even louder and more passionate attack on the vile morals of all Australians when there was a sound of brisk footsteps on the path.

'Good morning, all,' said Richard Daly cheerfully. 'I did ring the front doorbell, but nobody seemed to hear me.'

Mario cast one vicious glance at the new arrival and rolled his eyes almost into the back of his head.

'Porca miseria!' he muttered under his breath. 'It's you, is it?'

Richard could not have been unaware of such venomous hostility, but it seemed to make no impression on him whatsoever. He greeted Lisa smilingly, complimented Sandra on her clothes and sniffed appreciatively at the coffee.

'That smells good,' he remarked casually, sitting opposite Sandra. 'Have you got a cup to spare, Mrs Calvi?'

'Lisa,' she corrected him with a friendly smile.

Mario snorted as he watched this scoundrel being plied with coffee and croissants. 'That's fine,' he growled. 'Offer him coffee, offer him pastries, invite him to breakfast. Why not? Maybe you'd also like to take my sister upstairs to bed while you're at it, Dr Daly?'

Lisa winced and Sandra held her breath. But Richard did not seem in the least put out by this extraordinary suggestion.

'Ah,' he replied serenely. 'Tempting as the invitation is, I'm afraid I must decline, at least for today. Sandra and I have other plans.'

His eyes darted across to Sandra's. Tawny and gleaming, they held a sparkle of amusement, but also something else—a glittering refusal to be bullied.

'Oh,' said Mario through his teeth. 'So if you are not planning to go to bed with my sister, may I ask what you were doing kissing her in my front garden last night?'

Richard swallowed a morsel of croissant and dabbed his lips with a napkin.

'No, you may not,' he replied pleasantly. 'It's none of your damned business.'

Mario turned purple.

'I see,' he rasped. 'And I suppose you'll tell me that these plans you and Sandra have for today are none of my business either?'

Richard examined the remains of his croissant thoughtfully and poured himself a glass of orange juice. He either did not see or chose to ignore the frantic warning signals that Sandra was making at him across the table.

'Oh, I wouldn't say that,' he conceded generously. 'You'll have to know sooner or later anyway. I'm taking Sandra to an interview for a nursing job at the Nelson Hospital.'

There was a moment's hushed silence. Then Mario's fist crashed on the table, setting the glasses rattling.

'No!' he thundered. 'No, no and no! I forbid it, Sandra, do you hear me? I will not permit you to go.'

Sandra opened her mouth to speak, but before she could say a word Richard broke in. His eyes were gleaming and there was an alert, challenging twist to his lips. It was clear that he was enjoying every moment of this confrontation.

'But it's not up to you to decide, is it?' he asked silkily. 'Sandra's a grown woman. She can make up her own mind what she wants to do, can't she?'

'Yes, I can,' announced Sandra tartly. 'And you'd do well to remember it too, Richard! I don't need either of you telling me what to do. If I want to stay in Sydney, I'll do it, but it's my choice. I'm an independent woman! Do you understand?'

Mario dismissed that argument with a splutter of contempt and a flourishing wave of the hand.

'Independent woman!' he snorted. 'There's

no such thing! I understand you better than you think, Sandra. You only want to stay in Sydney because you've fallen head over heels in love with this worthless son of a—'

'Mario!' cut in Sandra furiously. 'That's ridiculous! I told you yesterday morning that I wanted to stay in Sydney, and I hadn't even met Richard then. So how can being in love with him have anything to do with it?'

She glimpsed Richard's sly grin and blushed with embarrassment.

'Not that I am anyway!' she added hastily.

Outfoxed by her logic, Mario chose to ignore it. Instead he concentrated his fire on Richard. Brandishing his bread and butter-knife, he waved it threateningly in the other man's face.

'Stop trying to talk her into staying here!' he demanded. 'You're only doing it for your own selfish reasons, and you'll end up ruining her life. Sandra has always been perfectly happy travelling with the family in the past, and we can't manage without her. My son Tony depends on her for everything.'

'Exactly!' retorted Richard crisply. 'And

59

that's a situation which is bad for both of them. Tony is not Sandra's son and she's being asked to carry far too much responsibility for him. What's more, I must tell you, as a haematologist, that it would be far better for your son to live in one place, close to good medical care. By dragging him round the world like this you're putting his health at risk. Maybe even his life.'

'How dare you say that?' roared Mario. 'Tony has had a private nurse from the moment he was born. Whenever Sandra was not available I have always hired somebody else as a substitute. That boy has never been left alone for a minute!'

'Which is probably why he's giving everybody such a hard time!' pointed out Richard. 'He needs to go to school and have as normal a life as he can, within limits, not be dragged around with grown-ups the entire time. No wonder he tried to give Sandra the slip yesterday. The poor little wretch must be bored senseless.'

'So now you're telling me how to raise my son, are you?' demanded Mario. 'Well, look here, il Dottor Daly—'

'No, you look here!' cut in Richard. 'I don't know how much you really understand about haemophilia, Mr Calvi, but your son has a very severe case of it. He has less than one per cent of Factor VIII in his blood, which means that he's liable to suffer bleeding into joints and muscles after quite minor injury. He could even suffer bleeding into the brain after something as mild as a tooth extraction.'

'Tony has never suffered any injury worse than the one he had yesterday,' muttered Mario defensively. 'And that's all completely under control.'

'Yes!' snapped Richard. 'Because he was close to a good hospital with adequate supplies of blood. But just supposing he cuts himself while you're in transit on an international flight; what then? He could bleed to death in the time it would take to reach the next airport! Or what if he needs a blood transfusion in a country where screening of blood products isn't as effective as it is in Australia? Since screening of blood products began in May 1985, Australia has had no known case of HIV being transmitted by transfusion. But not all countries are so careful or so fortunate. Your son's illness is serious, Mr Calvi, and your responsibility to him doesn't begin and end with providing a private nurse. If you'd like to come and see me at the hospital some time, I'd be happy to discuss the subject further with you.'

Mario made a rude noise.

'I will not be coming to discuss that subject or any other with you, il Dottor Daly,' he retorted. 'I am flying to New York on Tuesday morning and as soon as Tony is well enough to travel he will come and join me. And so will Sandra!'

Richard raised his eyebrows mockingly.

'Will you, Sandra?' he demanded.

Both men watched her searchingly as they waited for her reply. But while Mario's expression was a mixture of rage and anxiety Richard's face showed nothing but a calm, infuriating confidence. At that moment Sandra almost hated him. She would have liked to wipe the smile off his face, but the whole issue was too important for spite. Slowly and reluctantly she shook her head.

'No,' she said huskily. 'I'm sorry, Mario, but I won't be coming. And I hope you won't take Tony either. I know Richard hasn't been very tactful about any of this, but what he's saying is true. Tony would be better off staying in one place near a good hospital.'

Mario's eyes flashed. 'So you're going to side with this scoundrel against your own family, are you?'

She gave an impatient sigh. 'It's not like that, Mario!' she began. 'Richard isn't—'

But Richard interrupted her.

'It's time we were leaving, Sandra,' he said crisply.

And, rising to his feet, he came round and pulled out her chair. With an unhappy glance at her brother, Sandra stood up.

'If you go with him, you're no sister of mine,' warned Mario furiously. 'I'll disown you!'

She paused with an anguished expression on her face, but Richard took no more notice than if a mosquito were annoying him.

'Go and get your bag,' he ordered. 'You're not going to let him blackmail you, remember?'

With a last pleading look at Mario Sandra vanished into the house. When she returned with her bag a moment later Lisa cast a defiant glare at her husband and kissed Sandra on the cheek.

'Good luck,' she whispered.

But when Sandra moved hesitantly

towards Mario he turned his head deliberately away and stared out at the harbour. Biting her lip, she hurried up the path after Richard.

'Is he always as sweet-tempered as this?' asked Richard as the car purred quietly away down the road.

Sandra's confused emotions boiled over.

'Oh, shut up!' she flared. 'Half of it was your doing anyway. Couldn't you have been a bit more diplomatic about it?'

He gave a rueful chuckle. 'Have you ever known diplomacy to work with Mario?' he asked.

Sandra pulled a face. 'No,' she admitted unwillingly. Then tears pricked her eyes. 'But he's my brother and I'm very fond of him.'

Richard sighed.

'And I do him the justice of believing that he's very fond of you,' he replied. 'But I still don't think he's got any right to run your life for you and tell you what to do.'

'Oh, and you have, have you?' she retorted. 'Is there really any difference between you and Mario? You just hijacked me this morning! If you ask me, there's not a penny to choose between the pair of you when it comes to manipulating people.'

He winced.

'That's different,' he said obstinately. 'I'm helping you to do what you really want to do!'

Sandra pulled out a handkerchief and blew her nose. 'I suppose so,' she admitted gloomily. 'But I wish it didn't have to involve upsetting Mario so much. He's been wonderful to me, you know, especially since our father died.'

'When was that?' asked Richard.

'Ten years ago. I was only sixteen at the time. Mamma just went to pieces. She wanted to move back to Italy and take me with her, but I was horrified at the idea. Luckily Mario and Lisa invited me to live with them, so Mamma went back to Orvieto and I stayed on in Australia. It wasn't easy for them. Lisa was pregnant and Mario wasn't rich or well-known in those days, but they always made me feel welcome. And Mario paid for me to finish school and do my nursing training. I really owe him a lot.'

'Oh, love and guilt!' exclaimed Richard in exasperation. 'Where would families be without them? But don't get your knickers in a twist about Mario. I'm sure he'll come round.'

'Are you?' asked Sandra in a tremulous voice.

'Yes!' he growled. 'Now for heaven's sake look a bit more cheerful. The ADON is never going to believe you want to work at the Nelson if you turn up with a face like that. You look as if you're applying for a job in the salt mines!'

Richard's lack of sympathy infuriated Sandra. Obviously her first impression of him had been only too accurate. He was callous, insensitive and high-handed. So why on earth was she in this car with him on her way to a job which would only cause even more trouble? Because I'm stupid, she thought. Stupid and wimpish and easily overruled by domineering males. I should have told him to push off.

'What is it?' demanded Richard, glimpsing her morose expression. 'What are you thinking?'

'That I'm stupid and wimpish and easily overruled by domineering males,' she said sourly.

'Yes, you are,' he agreed. 'You should have told Mario to push off years ago.'

'That wasn't what I meant!' snapped Sandra. 'You're the domineering male I was thinking of!'

'I'm flattered,' he retorted silkily.

She cast him a smouldering took, but he only laughed. Outside the shoreline was flashing past and there were long stretches of oleander hedges waving their pink and white flowers against the dark blue backdrop of the ocean. Seagulls soared by in the dazzling sunlight and the surf broke on long white beaches shaded by Norfolk Island pines. It was impossible to go on feeling miserable or angry in such surroundings. When Richard turned into the driveway of the Nelson Hospital Sandra felt an unwilling thrill of excitement course through her.

'Well,' said Richard with a challenging look, 'are you ready for the start of a whole new life?'

CHAPTER FOUR

'I'm afraid all the ADONs are pretty busy this morning,' Richard explained as they crossed the car park. 'But Jane Carlton says she can see you at eleven-thirty. That gives us a fair bit of time to kill, so I thought you might like me to give you an unofficial tour of the hospital first.'

'All right,' agreed Sandra grudgingly.

The moment she was inside the building the familiar smell of disinfectant and floor polish, the sight of nurses in crisp blue and white uniforms and the faint rumble of trolleys acted on her like a drug. She followed Richard around in a pleasant daze while he showed her everything from the casualty section to airy wards overlooking the sea, operating theatres, a dispensary, linen-rooms, kitchens, nurses' stations, a large staff cafeteria and finally his own empire in the haematology section. Stopping outside a door with a sign saying 'DR RICHARD DALY, HAEMATOLOGIST', he turned the handle and ushered her into a large, airy room.

'Now, if you'd like to park yourself in a chair for a minute, I'll just go and collect my mail and be right back,' he assured her.

Left alone, Sandra gazed around her. Immediately in front of her was a huge desk, covered in a litter of papers, and the wall behind it was divided up by two large windows. Every other available piece of space seemed to be covered by shelves or large items of medical equipment. Books and journals crammed every inch, and on the top row of shelves there was a rather gruesome collection of glass jars containing organs pickled in formalin. A large microscope in a plastic cover held pride of place on the desk and there was a mountain of correspondence in the out-tray and an even bigger mountain in the in-tray. Obviously Richard Daly was a very busy man.

Picking her way across to the one available armchair, Sandra looked down doubtfully at a pile of journals that were stacked precariously on it. Perhaps she could lift them up without disturbing anything. But when she tried the whole pile collapsed in an avalanche on the floor. She was still on her hands and knees picking up copies of *Blood, Serials in Haematology, The American Journal of Dermopathology* and *Australian Power-Boating* when the door opened and Richard came back into the room.

'I do like to see women fall on their knees before me with adoring looks on their faces,' he teased, helping her to her feet.

She threw him a look that was anything but adoring.

'This place is a total mess,' she said severely. 'One of these days somebody will trip over your junk and have a nasty accident in here.'

'You're probably right,' he agreed, flinging a copy of *Ham's Histology* carelessly on to his desk. 'But at least the dashing Dr Daly will be here to come to their aid when it happens, not to mention the resources of a fine blood bank. And, while we're on the subject of blood banks, how about a quick cup of coffee and then I'll take you in to have a look at our set-up? Considering your interest in haemophilia, you'd probably like to see how they do the cross-matching of blood.'

'All right. Thanks,' agreed Sandra.

The staff-room was a casual, relaxed place, full of comfortable armchairs and painted a sunny yellow colour. Somebody's discarded lab coat hung carelessly over a radiator and the notice board was covered with signs about staff tennis matches and social events, as well as the usual medical posters. Sandra grinned as she glanced idly at the largest notice of all. Nothing to do with cardio-pulmonary resuscitation or hazardous chemicals, it was printed in huge straggling red letters and said, 'OK, WHO OWES THE CHOCKIE-BOX MONEY? WE'RE $6 SHORT, SO EITHER COUGH UP OR THERE WILL BE NO MORE CHOCKIE BICKIES FOR MORNING TEA!' Evidently the delinquent was still at large, for there was nothing but a handful of biscuits in the tin when Sandra reached it.

Most of the staff had already finished their morning tea, but a few people were sitting around nursing mugs and chatting. Richard introduced her to several of them and then led her to a quiet table in a corner.

'Well, how do you like the look of the place?' he asked, taking a swift gulp of coffee.

'You must have an asbestos throat to do that,' said Sandra in horror. 'Aren't you afraid you'll burn yourself?'

He grinned wickedly. 'You sound like a wife,' he marvelled. 'First it's, "Tidy up your room, Richard!" And now it's "Drink your coffee slowly, Richard!" I'm surprised you didn't read me a lecture about hot liquids and throat cancer.'

71

Sandra flushed. 'I'm sorry,' she said stiffly.

'Don't be,' he murmured. 'I rather like it. It's years since I've had anybody to nag me.'

His golden-brown eyes were fixed warmly on her and she was conscious of an odd, tremulous feeling in the pit of her stomach. Somehow the most extraordinary intimacy seemed to have sprung up between them from the first moment they met. Perhaps it was because Richard always said exactly what he thought, however outrageous. And now she was doing exactly the same thing.

'It's your fault,' she retorted. 'You're awfully outspoken yourself, so it's probably contagious.'

He winced. 'All right,' he agreed in a resigned voice. 'I'll take the blame for it, but you still haven't answered my question. How do you like the hospital? Do you think you'll want to work here?'

Sandra stared reflectively into her cup.

'I love it,' she said simply. 'I'll be able to get heaps of experience working on the wards, which is just what I want. Besides, the staff are friendly and there seems to be a really good social life out of hours.'

And I'll be near you, she added silently.

Yet although she did not say it aloud she couldn't help wondering if Richard had read her thoughts, he was watching her face so intently.

'Good,' he replied curtly. 'On your feet, then, and we'll go and see the blood bank.'

Sandra's emotions were in turmoil as she followed him along the corridor with its buttercup-yellow walls and its paraphernalia of rosters, trolleys, fire-extinguishers and other hospital clutter. She wished she knew what Richard's real feelings were towards her. Was he just flirting mildly with her, or did he feel the same deep, unsettling attraction that she felt towards him? But the question had to go unanswered as he came to a halt outside a room with an impressive official signpost saying 'Blood Bank' above the door. Plastered to the wall below it was an unofficial sign with a cartoon of a leering, black-bearded male holding a placard saying, 'RIPPER THE STRIPPER AND HIS GLORIOUS CHORUS'. The man in the cartoon was surrounded by a bevy of beautiful women wearing veils and very little else. Sandra was riveted to the spot with curiosity, but Richard barely seemed to notice. He poked his head around the door.

'Hi, Barry,' he said. 'Is it OK if I bring in a visitor?'

'Sure. Come on in, mate.'

Barry bore such an uncanny resemblance to the character in the cartoon that Sandra almost doubled up with laughter. He was a huge, burly man with a riot of black curly hair and a black beard, dressed in a white hospital gown and wearing rubber gloves. His four female assistants, similarly attired but much prettier, were grouped around a large aluminium table covered with racks of test-tubes.

'Now, let me introduce you,' said Richard. 'This is Sandra Calvi, who's a nurse and is thinking of coming to work for us here.' And Sandra, left to right these are Marie Collins, Jenny Buckland, Roseanne Finch, Louise Graham and Barry Ripper. Barry, Sandra has a particular interest in haemophilia, so I wondered if you could show her how you cross-match blood here?'

'Sure,' agreed Barry.

He walked across to one of the huge aluminium refrigerators by the wall and drew out a bag of blood.

'It's pretty straightforward,' he said. 'To cross-match donor blood against the patient's serum we just place a certain volume of serum and a certain volume of donor blood in test tubes, incubate it at thirty-seven degrees Centigrade for ten minutes, then spin it and look for agglutination. Now, is there anything else I can tell you about our work here?'

'Yes,' said Sandra with a dimple of amusement. 'I'd like to know about the RIPPER THE STRIPPER sign outside the door.'

Richard gave a groan of mock horror. 'She lowers the tone of the place, doesn't she?' he demanded.

Barry winked at Sandra. 'Yeah, definitely,' he agreed. 'But not half as much as I do, mate. Well, I'll tell you about that, Sandra. When you get to know Richard better, you'll find out that he's a fundraising demon. You can't even afford to stop and count your change in the cafeteria, because he'll snap it up right under your nose and put it into the fund for his latest bit of equipment. What he's got his heart set on at the moment is a coagulometer, which will cost him about forty thousand pounds. It does factor assays and it's really handy for diagnosing disorders like haemophilia and ensuring that treatment is adequate. Anyway, he decided he'd organise a hospital theatre revue last year to raise money. After he twisted our arms a bit the girls and I volunteered to put on a sketch. What I originally had in mind was for the girls to do a bit of belly-dancing. Well, what's the point of being surrounded by all these gorgeous women if they won't take, their clothes off? But they turned out to be real spoilsports, so...' he paused dramatically and flung his arms wide '...Ripper the Stripper was born!' he finished triumphantly.

Sandra gazed at his enormous bulk in awe.

'You don't mean that you—?' she began.

'Oh, yes, mate. And it was a terrific success. One thing you've got to admit—if you come to see Barry Ripper belly-dancing, you really get to see some belly! The crowds loved it. Especially when I got down to my fluorescent green underpants! I'll tell you, Sandra, there were women swooning with desire in the aisles.'

'Choking with laughter, more like it,' muttered Louise.

Barry fixed her with an indignant glare.

'Take no notice of her, Sandra,' he said with dignity. 'It's nothing but professional jealousy. Anyway, if you'd like to be involved in this year's revue, just give Richard a buzz. We're always on the look-out for new talent.'

Sandra was still giggling as Richard led her away down the corridor.

'Isn't he priceless?' she laughed.

'Barry? Yes, he's a great bloke. Very good at his job, too. And he's absolutely right about the revue, if you'd like to take part. Surely with that Calvi background you must have some kind of secret longing to tread the boards?'

Sandra smiled.

'I hate to admit this,' she replied, 'but I can't even sing in tune. Although I suppose you're right in a way. When I was younger I did sometimes wish that I could be in the limelight too. Still, on the whole, I think I'm really more the type to hang about in the wings, soothing the prima donnas.'

'Well, you can do that if you like,' agreed Richard. 'We need somebody to handle the props and so on. Good lord, is that the time? You'd better come back to my room and pick up your things for the interview.'

Sandra was looking decidedly gloomy as he unlocked the door to his room.

'What's the matter?' he asked. 'You haven't got cold feet, have you?'

'Yes. No. I don't know,' she replied incoherently.

His hands descended on her shoulders, large and warm and comforting. 'Tell me what's wrong,' he urged. 'Have I pushed you too hard?'

Sandra smiled wryly. 'Not exactly,' she said. 'I'm quite certain that I want to work here, but I'm nervous about the interview. And I'm utterly appalled at the thought of what Mario's going to say if I do get the job.'

Richard's thumbs moved caressingly over her tense muscles.

'Wendy Jessup was right about you,' he remarked.

'What do you mean?' she demanded, thinking how blissful his fingers felt and yet wishing he would stop touching her.

'She told me you were far too loyal and reliable for your own good,' he replied. 'She also said that if you didn't break out and make a life of your own soon you'd still be playing the devoted spinster aunt ten years from now.'

'Oh, did she?' retorted Sandra indignantly.

'Mm,' agreed Richard provocatively. 'Frightening prospect, isn't it? Of course, you can avoid that dreadful fate by taking a job at the Nelson.'

'Stop trying to manipulate me!' she complained. 'It won't work.'

'All right, then, I'll try to bribe you instead,' he replied. 'If you stop worrying about Mario and go to your interview, I'll take you out to dinner on Saturday week. How about that?'

'What?' she exclaimed in a startled voice.

Richard winked. 'Think it over and give me an answer later,' he urged. 'Now come on, we've got to get moving. And don't look so petrified. Jane Carlton is a very nice woman.'

Jane Carlton was a very nice woman. When Sandra entered the ADON's office five minutes later she found a motherly-looking, grey-haired woman writing busily with her head down, half hidden by a stack of papers. Looking up, she gave Sandra a cheerful smile.

'Miss Calvi, isn't it?' she said. 'I'm Sister Carlton. Do come in and sit down. I'm so sorry about this paperwork. Every time I get these wretched rosters straight somebody comes down sick and I have to start over from scratch.'

She heaved the pile of papers to one side and looked at Sandra piercingly over the top of her glasses.

'Right. Now tell me all about yourself,' she urged briskly. 'Dr Daly said you trained at Royal North Shore. Is that correct?'

'Yes,' agreed Sandra hesitantly, producing a folder of documents. 'I've got my certificates here, if you'd like to see them.'

Sister Carlton took the folder and perused it. Her eyebrows rose.

'Excellent exam results!' she said with a hearty chuckle. 'Obviously you worked a great deal harder than I did when I was a student nurse.' She glanced surreptitiously at a handwritten paper in front of her. 'Dr Daly has also explained to me how you've been taking care of your haemophiliac nephew over the past four years, but I believe you've also had some hospital experience in that time as well. Could you just tell me about that?'

'Yes, Sister,' agreed Sandra, clearing her throat. 'When I finished my training I worked full time at Royal North Shore for a year. After that I always spent at least four months of each year in Australia, and I used to do relief work during that time. I've also done some work in various New York hospitals on a part-time basis, as you can see from my curriculum vitae. My references from the New York hospitals are in the folder too.'

Sister Carlton nodded thoughtfully.

'And you've kept up your registration as a nurse in New South Wales?'

'Yes, Sister.'

'Tell me, do you hold any post-basic nursing qualifications? Or are you working towards any?'

'I have my Accident and Emergency Certificate—I got that at Royal North Shore. That's all so far, but I'd like to qualify in Paediatrics if I get the chance.'

'And why do you want to work at the Nelson Hospital?' demanded Sister Carlton.

The question shot out so abruptly that it caught Sandra off guard. She could do nothing but blurt out the truth.

'Because I love hospital work and I'm sick and tired of travelling,' she replied candidly.

The older woman pursed her lips and nodded.

'Your background is a little unusual,' she pointed out. 'But that won't necessarily be held against you.'

She asked Sandra a few more questions about her training and experience and outlined the hospital routine to her. At last she shuffled her papers together and inspected her once more over the top of her glasses. Sandra twisted her hands together and gazed back anxiously. Sister Carlton looked inscrutable for a moment and then relented.

'Could you possibly start the day after tomorrow?' she asked.

Sandra beamed. 'Yes, please!' she replied fervently.

When she came out of the office, she found that Richard was waiting for her. His tawny eyes searched her face.

'How did it go?' he asked.

She took a deep, unsteady breath.

'Well, I've taken the plunge,' she said. 'I start on Wednesday at seven a.m.'

'Are you pleased?' he probed.

'Yes, I suppose so,' she agreed.

And she was. Yet somehow the prospect also made her feel desperately uneasy.

The next twenty-four hours were a very tense time in the Calvi household. Although Mario did not actually carry out his threat to disown Sandra he left her in no doubt that he was furious about her decision to take the hospital job. With Tony still in hospital there could be no question of the entire family flying to New York. But as he left for the airport on Tuesday evening Mario summed up his feelings dramatically.

'You might have won the first battle, Sandra,' he shouted from the car window, 'but I'll win the war! I'll be back in a couple of months and then we'll get this nonsense sorted out once and for all!'

Yet when Lisa returned from the airport she was philosophical.

'A lot can happen in two months, Sandra,' she pointed out when they were brewing their hot chocolate at bedtime. 'As soon as Tony comes out of hospital tomorrow I'm going to enrol him at the same school as William Jessup. If Mario sees that he's settled in and making friends, perhaps he'll realise that it's not a good idea to disturb him. Besides, in six weeks you might have quite a little romance going with this handsome Dr Daly, eh?'

Sandra snorted.

'What makes you so sure he has romance in mind?' she retorted sceptically.

Lisa clicked her tongue.

'Why else would he kidnap you and take you out to dinner like that?' she demanded. 'And why else would he come and drag you off to that job interview? I've never seen anything so romantic in my life! You take my word for it, Sandra. Richard Daly wanted you to work at the Nelson Hospital for one reason and one reason only—because he's crazy about you. I can see it in his eyes. And I wouldn't be a bit surprised if we're eating the wedding candies by the end of the year!'

CHAPTER FIVE

But if Richard Daly really was crazy about Sandra he kept his passion well hidden during the rest of the week. On her first day she was kept busy at an orientation programme and the only glimpse she had of Richard was in the

84

hospital cafeteria at lunchtime. His red-gold hair stood out unmistakably in the crowd and, with her heartbeat quickening, Sandra chose a route which would take her directly past his table. Yet if she hoped he would invite her to join him she was disappointed. He acknowledged her presence only with a quick upward movement of his head and immediately returned to his conversation with the woman beside him. As unobtrusively as she could Sandra took a quick glance at her. Dark, glossy hair cut in a flawless bell shape, magnolia-pale skin and the kind of make-up that took a *Vogue* model three hours to achieve. The badge on her white lab coat said, 'DR FELICITY HAMILTON'.

Conscious of Sandra's scrutiny, the other woman looked up. Her dark eyes flicked over Sandra's blue nursing uniform in a swift, contemptuous movement, then, with a look of amusement, she turned back to Richard.

'Tell me more about the hospital ball, darling,' she urged lazily, laying one hand on his arm.

Something about both the look and the gesture made Sandra fume. Perhaps she was imagining things, but she felt certain she could interpret both. The scornful glance said, 'Oh, that ridiculous little nurse is in love with Richard. How funny!' And the hand on the arm said, 'He's my property. Keep off!' The worst of it was that Richard did nothing to contradict either of those claims.

Gritting her teeth, Sandra sat down at a distant table and began unloading her salad, wholemeal roll, yoghurt and juice. She was just attacking a piled of grated carrot with her fork when a hand fell on her shoulder.

'Sandra Calvi!' said an astonished voice. 'It is you! I thought it was, the moment I came in the door. Bet you don't remember me! We did our training together at Royal North Shore.'

Sandra glanced up and saw a tall, buxom girl with auburn hair and a wide smile. The face was immediately familiar, but the name took her a moment longer.

'Of course I remember you!' she exclaimed. 'Laura, isn't it? Laura Madden?'

'Maddox,' corrected Laura. 'But listen, what are you doing here? I heard you had some glamorous job, swanning around the world with your haemophiliac nephew.'

'I did,' agreed Sandra. 'But I got sick of it and gave it up.'

Laura pulled an astonished face, but before she could reply a couple of hospital porters with trays edged their way apologetically past her.

'Do sit down,' urged Sandra. 'I'm afraid you'll be sent flying there. Besides, I want to hear what you've been up to.'

Ten minutes' concentrated chatter revealed that Laura had been doing hospital work ever since she had finished her training, that she had not married that swine Phil Webster whom she had been engaged to, that the Nelson was a really great place to work and that she was throwing a big party at her flat on Saturday week.

'Why don't you come, Sandra?' she urged, peeling the foil off her custard. 'You could meet heaps of people who work here and start making some new friends.'

Sandra smiled. 'Thanks, Laura,' she said regretfully. 'Any other time I'd love to, but I've got a date that Saturday.'

Laura looked interested.

'Lucky you!' she commented. 'Anybody I know?'

'Yes, actually,' agreed Sandra. 'It's Richard Daly, the haematologist. He works here.'

Laura gave a soft whistle.

'Richard Daly!' she exclaimed enviously. 'That man's so sexy, half the nursing staff at the Nelson are in love with him. Where on earth did you meet him?'

Swiftly Sandra described her chance encounter with Richard three days earlier. A rapt look spread over Laura's face.

'How romantic!' she breathed. 'Ooh, I do love masterful men. But you ought to be careful with Richard Daly, Sandra.'

Sandra looked startled. 'Why?' she demanded bluntly.

'Well, he's a real charmer,' admitted Laura. 'But I don't think he's the kind of bloke that's interested in settling down. Nobody really knows much about his background, but he's generally regarded as a bit of a womaniser. As a matter of fact, you're not a bit like the kind of woman he usually goes around with.'

Hating herself for indulging in this sort of gossip, Sandra leaned forward confidentially.

'What kind of woman is that?' she asked with elaborate carelessness.

Laura wrinkled her nose critically.

'The high-fliers,' she said. 'The man-eaters. Glossy and glamorous and hard as nails—like her!'

She cast a withering glance down the cafeteria to the table at the far end where Felicity Hamilton was still sitting opposite Richard. Even at this distance there was a strong aura of intimacy about the gold head and the dark one, so close together. Sandra felt a chill of dismay strike through her. Was Richard just amusing himself by flirting mildly with her, when all the time his real interest lay in women like Dr Hamilton? Suddenly the fruity sourness of her yoghurt no longer seemed to appetising. She pushed the half-finished tub away.

'Yes, well, it's only dinner, isn't it?' she retorted briskly, rising to her feet. 'I wasn't actually expecting him to propose this weekend.'

Laura grimaced.

'I'm sorry,' she said. 'I didn't mean to offend you. Look, you will come round to the flat some other night for a meal, won't you?'

Sandra forced a smile.

'Yes, of course,' she agreed remorsefully.

'But I must go now. It's been really nice seeing you again.'

'And you,' replied Laura. 'Anyway, it might be all rubbish, the things people say about him.'

'Yes, it might,' said Sandra firmly.

Yet as she walked away, with her head held high, a flood of doubts came sweeping through her. Or it might not, she thought grimly. As she passed Richard's table she glanced hopefully at him, but he acknowledged her with no more than a brief upturning of his lips. Despair crept through her, but she walked on with apparent serenity. Whatever happened she was not going to give that awful Felicity Hamilton the chance to gloat over her.

Once in the relative privacy of the hospital corridors she reflected bitterly over Laura's words. Should she phone Richard and cancel their plans for dinner? But if she did what on earth was she to say? 'Laura Maddox says you're an absolute womaniser and I'm simply too much of a wimp to risk eating in your company. Boo-hoo!' No, she would only make herself look ridiculous. All she could do was to stay on her guard whenever she found herself with Richard.

That proved to be a depressingly easy task in the days that followed. After her orientation programme Sandra was assigned to a women's surgical ward, and the only times she saw Richard were when he came through, shortly before eight a.m., on his ward rounds. Since she was rushing frantically to complete the early routine of injections, medications, IV fluid charts and patients' breakfasts, she was in no condition to exchange melting glances with him. And Richard himself was completely professional. Although he had a pleasant manner with patients he had a reputation for blistering sarcasm over sloppy work. All the nurses were on their toes during his visits, and there was a general sigh of relief when he departed. In fact, his only conversation with Sandra during working hours consisted of a stiff reprimand for failing to label a blood bottle immediately after taking a sample, followed by her stammering apology.

Yet the memory of that long, sensual kiss in the moonlight kept straying back at the worst possible moments to disturb her. And, as she came off duty each afternoon, she found her heartbeat quickening with the half-formed hope that Richard would be waiting for her. But he never was. When she was finally hailed on Friday afternoon as she emerged into the car park it was not Richard who approached her. It was Barry.

'Just the girl I wanted to see!' he exclaimed without preamble. 'Listen, what are you doing tonight, love?'

Sandra stared at the burly, black-bearded technician with a startled expression. Barry was an awfully nice fellow, but there was no way that she could feel any attraction to him. Her thoughts must have shown in her face, for Barry suddenly let out a loud guffaw.

'It's all right, mate,' he reassured her. 'I'm not about to make some sleazy kind of pass at you. I reckon my missus would belt me over the head with a frying-pan if I tried. No, what I'm here about is our revue. You did say you'd be interested in joining in, and we're in a bit of a fix at the moment. Marie Collins's husband has just got transferred north to Brisbane at short notice and she's had to pull out. If you could come to the rehearsal tonight and just read her part, it would really help us. We're trying to organise the lighting tonight and nobody else is available to fill in.'

Sandra smiled. 'All right,' she agreed warmly. 'What time?'

'Eight o'clock, main lecture theatre. We should be finished by ten, unless Richard gets a bee in his bonnet about something not being perfect.'

'Oh. Richard's going to be there, is he?'

'Yeah. Why? Is something wrong?'

'No. No, of course not,' she replied uneasily.

She wasn't at all sure that she wanted to see Richard again. Yet when she entered the main lecture theatre promptly at eight o'clock a pang of disappointment went through her as she saw that he wasn't there. Ten minutes passed, as others straggled in, but there was still no sign of Richard. At last Barry clapped his hands decisively.

'Right. We'll have to start without him,' he said. 'Sandra, take a look through this script, will you? Now, you're a TV presenter, doing a documentary on Medicare and government funding, right? All you've got to do is read out the commentary, completely deadpan, and take no notice of what the other actors are doing around you. If you can manage not to laugh, all the better. OK, folks. As soon as you're ready.'

The script was unremarkable in itself. All Sandra had to do was read from a document written in bureaucratic jargon, explaining how government funding cuts would, ultimately produce a much better public health service. Where the comedy took place was in the behaviour of the team of lunatics behind her, who were acting out the recommendations of her report. Sandra cleared her throat and began.

'The government today announced plans for funding cuts of five million pounds per annum to Medicare. Speaking on national television, the Prime Minister denied accusations that the cult would lead to a down-grading of health care. He said that economies could be achieved by sharing equipment between major hospitals, by rationalising the frequency of home nursing visits and by using less costly forms of treatment where appropriate—'

Out of the corner of her eye she saw a flurry of activity towards the rear of the stage. Doctors dressed in stocking masks snatched an oxygen mask from a patient's face and fled out of the window, leaving him to die, a nurse making a home visit found she was staring at a skeleton, two ambulance officers wearing jackets labelled 'EMERGENCY ROAD TRAUMA SERVICE' skipped on stage, carrying a large box of Band-Aids. But all the years spent in famous theatres around the world had given Sandra a poise that she did not know she possessed. Without difficulty she controlled the urge to burst into giggles and kept reading. Halfway through she heard the sound of soft footsteps padding down the aisle, but she kept going smoothly. As she finished there was a spontaneous burst of applause from the other actors.

'You were terrific, mate!' roared Barry from the back of the theatre. 'Bloody marvellous!'

But the man whose approval Sandra really cared about was the golden-haired doctor who now sat staring at her from the front row of seats. As the lights came up she saw that Richard was leaning forward, scrutinising her intently.

'Is something wrong?' she asked uncomfortably.

'Wrong? No, Barry hit the nail on the head. You were marvellous! Listen, Sandra, I've just had a thought about another project you might be interested in. Could you spare me half an hour when this is over?'

Sandra's curiosity was piqued and, when the rehearsal was finally over, she stepped down off the stage and came to meet Richard.

'You said you wanted to talk to me?' she said hesitantly. 'About some project?'

'That's right,' he agreed, steering her skilfully through the throng of other people who were chatting and laughing around them. 'If you can come back to my office for a while, I'll tell you what it's about.'

He strode along the corridors so briskly that she almost had to run to keep up with him. His tawny eyes were alight with enthusiasm and his square chin was thrust out determinedly as he spoke.

'I've been asked to do a segment on a TV current affairs programme which is to be filmed quite soon,' he explained. 'It's about the blood donor programme. We always have a major problem keeping up adequate supplies in the blood bank, and a programme about our work is a real godsend. It's sure to send the number of volunteers shooting sky-high if it's handled correctly. But I have a problem.

'As you probably know, the Red Cross

Blood Transfusion Service takes all the blood donations and stores them in a central blood bank. Then they distribute them to hospitals, according to need. What the producer of the programme wants is a sort of overview from start to finish. First some shots of blood donors giving blood, then of the refrigerated vehicles delivering it to a typical hospital. After that they'll film Barry doing some cross-matching in our own blood bank, and finally there'll be some shots of patients actually receiving the blood in hospital. In order to tie it together they want somebody to give a running commentary on what's going on. That's easy enough, I can manage that. The only trouble is that the producer wants me to have a nurse along as my sidekick. Preferably somebody glamorous. That's why I thought of you.'

'Me?' echoed Sandra in a horrified voice. 'Why me?'

'Well, obviously you don't suffer from stage fright,' he pointed out. 'And of course, you also have the advantage of being very physically appealing. You're cute and blonde and fluffy, which will really help to pull in the viewers. All the men will find you irresistible.'

'Thanks!' retorted Sandra coldly.

'What's the matter now?' demanded Richard, unlocking his door and pushing it open with his shoulder. 'Why are you looking so offended? For heaven's sake, I just paid you a compliment!'

'A compliment that makes me feel like a piece of meat!' she sniffed. 'I don't want to be on television just so men can ogle me!'

He gave an exasperated sigh and snapped on the light. Waving her towards the armchair, he crossed to his desk.

'Women!' he said bitterly. 'I'll never understand them. I was just trying to tell you that I think you look terrific and you'd be great in the part. If I offended you, I'm sorry. But I'm too tired and, too hungry to figure out what I said that was wrong.'

Reaching across his desk, he pulled three or four plastic food containers towards him. 'Would it bother you awfully if I eat while we talk?' he asked, looking down at them ravenously. 'I've had nothing but a sandwich since lunchtime yesterday.'

'Why ever not?' demanded Sandra disapprovingly.

'Too busy,' replied Richard with a shrug. 'There was a major road accident last night just as I was going off duty. One of the victims had a very rare blood type and I called in help. Then I overslept this morning, snatched the sandwich about noon and I've been flat out ever since. That's why I'm starving.'

'I'm not surprised!' she exclaimed. 'Richard! For heaven's sake, you're not going to eat that stuff cold out of the container, are you?'

'Why not?' he retorted, with his plastic fork poised above a glutinous pink mess of honeyed prawns. 'I usually do.'

'There's a perfectly good microwave oven in the tearoom,' protested Sandra. 'Give it to me and I'll heat it up. It won't take a minute.'

In fact it took three minutes and, when she returned with a far more appetising arrangement of steaming Chinese food on a plate, she thought at first that Richard was asleep. He was sitting in the armchair with his eyes closed and his cheek propped on his hand. In the light from the desk-lamp Sandra could see lines of fatigue etched around his eyes and mouth. But the door squeaked as she kicked it shut behind her and he came to life. Sitting up with a start, he blinked and peered around him.

'You look worn out!' she said severely.

He shrugged.

'If I weren't worn out, I wouldn't be doing my job properly,' he replied.

'Don't be ridiculous!' she protested, handing him the plate.

Their fingers touched and she gave him an exasperated smile. He looked at her with his penetrating golden gaze and then he too smiled—a quirky, lop-sided smile that immediately banished any doubts she might have had about his character. That smile was far too sincere to be anything other than genuine.

'Have you had dinner?' he asked.

'No, I haven't, actually,' she admitted. 'I had to do some shopping when I finished work and there wasn't time.'

'Do you want to share?' he invited.

'There's only one plate,' she pointed out.

'I don't mind if you don't. And there's another fork somewhere here.'

'Well, those prawns do look good,' she agreed.

It could hardly compare with their candle-lit dinner the previous Sunday, and yet there was an extraordinary intimacy about it. The prawns were large and succulent, coated in crispy batter with a dusting of sesame seeds and smothered in a sweet, tangy plum sauce. And they were accompanied by a mound of savoury fried rice and a delectable concoction of chicken, baby corn and mangetout peas. It was one of the oddest and yet most satisfying meals Sandra had ever eaten. But in spite of a healthy appetite she scarcely seemed to make any impact on the vast mound of food, and it was left to Richard to finish it off.

'Oh, that was good,' he said at last with a satisfied sigh, looking down at the empty plate.

'Coffee?' asked Sandra.

'Please.'

When she came back he was sitting at his desk with a folder of notes open in front of him and a thoughtful frown on his face. But as she leaned forward to set his mug down he reached up and ruffled her hair.

'What would I do without you?' he demanded teasingly.

Sandra knew the words were only spoken playfully, and yet they sent a pang of emotion through her. It wasn't the first time she had eaten a makeshift meal with a doctor, but she felt as confused and vulnerable as any student nurse suffering from white-coat fever. She wasn't even sure that she liked Richard Daly, so why did she have this absurd impulse to return his caress? Backing nervously out of his grip, she reminded him of their purpose in being there.

'Shouldn't we get to work on this TV programme?' she asked him crisply.

He was studying her face thoughtfully and he did not answer at once. Then, with a sudden change of mood, he passed a set of notes to her.

'Yes, we should,' he agreed. 'Take a look through these and then I'll tell you what I have in mind.'

Sandra spent the next five minutes sipping her coffee and browsing through Richard's jottings. Then she looked up.

'Let me get this straight,' she said. 'You're going to start out at one of the Red Cross blood transfusion centres and get some footage of a donor giving blood. Is that right?'

'Yes, that's it.'

'But what exactly do you want me to do? Take the blood?'

'No. There would be problems with legal

liability if you did. All the Red Cross RNs are covered by Red Cross insurance in case of any mishaps, so one of their venipuncturists will deal with that. Your main role throughout the programme will be to provide reassurance. A lot of people are frightened of giving blood, so if you can make them feel happier about it you'll be doing a considerable service. What I thought you might do is help the blood donors fill in the forms, sit and chat to them while they're taking the blood, keep an eye on the bag and make sure the flow is correct. All that sort of thing. It will only be a standard four-thirty-ml donation, so it shouldn't take long.'

'I see,' agreed Sandra in a resigned voice. 'So I just sit and soothe their fevered brows, do I?'

'Something like that,' agreed Richard with a grin. 'And of course, if the TV journalist asks you any questions, be prepared to talk intelligently about what's going on, especially with regard to the transmission of AIDS and other infectious diseases via blood transfusions. Remember to stress that you can't catch AIDS by becoming a blood donor.'

'What about other diseases?' she asked.

'Is there anything else I should know about?'

He frowned.

'Well, they'll probably direct most of their questions to me,' he said. 'But if they do ask you, you ought to know that the incidence of other diseases transmitted by blood transfusions in Australia is negligible. Syphilis has never been transmitted in living memory, malaria hasn't been a problem for the last ten years and the risk of post-transfusion Hepatitis B is only about one in a hundred, a thousand in New South Wales. Donors are very carefully screened, and it's fair to say that giving blood is a very safe activity both for the donor and the patient who receives it. Once we get back to the Nelson Hospital we'll probably also get some footage of a patient receiving blood. Of course that depends on having a co-operative guinea-pig available on the day, but I might ask you to set up a drip for the benefit of the cameras. Do you think you can handle all that?'

'Yes, of course,' replied Sandra. 'When do you want me to do it?'

'I'll let you know when the TV station

gives me a firm date. Preferably on your rostered day off, but I'll be glad to reimburse you for your time.'

'I wouldn't think of it!' she retorted indignantly. 'I've had good reason to know how important the Blood Transfusion Service is, and I'd be only too happy to volunteer.'

'That's very generous of you,' said Richard. 'I thought I was being pretty smart in press-ganging you to come and work here, but now I'm sure of it.'

A shadow flitted over her face.

'Why were you so anxious for me to come and work here, Richard?' she asked impulsively. 'Was it just because the hospital is so short of nurses?'

She was conscious of a sudden tension in the room. Richard's face wore an uneasy look, as if he had just been cornered. Lifting his hand, he ran his fingers through his red-gold hair and gave a baffled sigh.

'Not exactly,' he admitted. 'I wouldn't have taken you out till two a.m., kissed you passionately in your front garden and then kidnapped you the following day merely because the hospital is short of nurses.'

Sandra gave a wry smile.

'It wasn't all part of some recruiting programme, then?' she said lightly. 'The hospital board didn't actually pay you a commission or anything?'

Richard gave a low growl of laughter.

'No, they didn't!' he retorted. 'But, now that you mention it, it sounds like a damned good idea. Maybe I ought to offer them my services to drum up more recruits.'

Sandra was silent for a moment, toying with one of her curls.

'Then why did you want me to stay?' she asked huskily.

'What a question!' he complained. 'I don't know. It just seemed like the obvious thing to do. There was no doubt in my mind that it would be better for Tony to stay in Sydney, I thought it was totally ridiculous for you to be wasting your nursing skills on one person, when you could be helping dozens, and...'

'And?' prompted Sandra.

'And you had the most glorious sapphire-blue eyes I'd ever seen,' finished Richard blandly.

With an impatient cry she rose to her feet and paced across the room. He went after her and his warm hands descended on her shoulders.

'What is it?' he demanded, turning her back to face him. 'Why are you looking so offended? Surely you must know that I found you devastatingly attractive right from the start?'

Sandra shrugged with annoyance. 'Don't be so glib!' she complained.

'Come on, Sandra!' he urged. 'It's the simple truth. I wanted you from the first moment I saw you. And I thought you felt the same way about me.'

I did, she thought grimly. I do. But she certainly wasn't going to make that admission.

'Please, Richard, don't!' she begged. 'I don't want to play silly games like this.'

And yet the slow, rhythmic caress of his warm hands on her shoulders was sending tremors of arousal quivering through her.

'It's no game, Sandra!' he said harshly. 'Meeting you was like being struck by lightning.'

She took in a long, shuddering breath and looked up at the relentless flame of his golden-brown eyes. There was no mistaking the urgency in them, and for one insane moment she was tempted to melt into his arms, to kiss him with all the warmth and passion that smouldered within her. In that instant she knew with painful certainty that she could easily fall in love with Richard Daly. But she was not at all sure that he even knew what love was. And what if this was no more than a shameless ploy to entice her into bed with him? She felt herself stiffen in his embrace.

'Don't you believe me?' he demanded hoarsely. 'No, I can see you don't. All right, Sandra. There's no need to panic. I know damned well what I'd like to do with you, and you know it too. I'd like to have you alone with me in the big bedroom at my place in the lamp-light. And I'd like to undress you very slowly and caress your naked body and hear you sigh very softly as I touched you. And I'd like to see that special, uncertain little smile around the corners of your mouth as I carried you to the bed. And then I'd make love to you, Sandra, and your eyes would shimmer, and after a while you'd lose all that earnest, serious control and go totally wild in my arms. I'd hear you whimpering and moaning under my touch, and I'd be more thrilled and aroused than I've ever been in my life. That's what I'd like, Sandra.'

She swallowed convulsively. 'W-would you?' she stammered in a high, unnatural voice.

Richard choked with laughter against her neck.

'Yes,' he murmured caressingly. 'But it's obvious you don't share my enthusiasm at the prospect. Yet. But I can wait for you, Sandra. I suppose I'll have to.'

She fixed her anguished blue eyes on him.

'Don't make fun of me, Richard,' she begged. 'I'm not into all this smart, sophisticated bed-hopping. When and if I make love with somebody, it has to have some meaning.'

'I'm beginning to realise that,' he agreed soberly, taking her hand and planting a kiss on the palm. 'Don't worry, Sandra, I'm not just playing games with you.'

He folded her fingers over, imprisoning the kiss.

'Now come on and I'll walk you to your car,' he added bracingly. 'And if what I've said tonight upsets you then just put it right out of your mind.'

That was more easily said than done, reflected Sandra ruefully, as they walked across the moonlit car park. There was no possible way she could forget Richard's husky words of desire, any more than she could forget that fervent kiss on her hand. She knew she ought to be outraged by both, and yet some fever seemed to be singing through her veins, so that she found her whole body aching with need. The truth was that she wanted Richard Daly every bit as badly as he wanted her. And if she was left alone with him long enough she had no doubt that she would soon surrender. The throbbing tide of passion would be too powerful for her to resist. I might lose my head at any moment, she thought apprehensively, then gave a small, unconscious wriggle as she realised how delicious the prospect was. Richard's arm tightened around her waist, but when they reached her car he did not kiss her as she expected. Instead he simply touched her cheek with a caressing gesture.

'Drive safely,' he said. 'And tell Lisa to bring young Tony in to be enrolled in our haemophiliacs' programme whenever it suits her.'

CHAPTER SIX

The following week Sandra took advantage of that invitation. While Mario was away she was anxious to get Tony as firmly established as possible in Sydney. And Lisa certainly needed no urging, although she did insist on having Sandra accompany her.

'You know how my English is, Sandra,' she coaxed. 'It's all right for most things, but when it comes to medical stuff I don't understand more than one word in ten that the doctors tell me. This way you'll be able to explain it all to me later.'

Thus is was that Sandra and Lisa found themselves in the haematology building a few days later. For the initial interview Tony was not to be present, although a battery of tests would be done on the boy at a later date. At Sandra's tentative knock Richard opened his office door and removed some journals from a couple of chairs so that they could both sit down.

'Hello, Lisa,' he said, shaking hands

warmly. 'How's young Tony?'

'Very well, thank you,' replied Lisa. 'He's going to school with Wendy Jessup's son now and he's thrilled to bits about it.'

'Good,' approved Richard. 'Well, take a pew and we'll talk about our comprehensive care programme for haemophiliacs. In the first place, do you have any idea of what that actually means?'

'No,' replied Lisa frankly.

'How about you, Sandra?' asked Richard.

'Yes, I think so,' she agreed. 'I've had some dealings with a similar project in New York, but it's probably best if you can just explain what happens here at the Nelson Hospital.'

Richard pressed his fingertips together. 'Well, it's a system that attempts to deal with the overall health care of haemophiliacs,' he explained. 'It's called by different names in different places, but basically what it comes down to is this. When a hospital has a programme of this kind in place, a haemophiliac can be registered with it and all his health details go on computer. Once every six months he comes in for a check-up and he has the chance to see the members of our haemophilia team. This includes a paediatrician, orthopaedist, occupational therapist, dentist, nurse, social worker and, later on, a vocational counsellor and genetic counsellor. None of us works solely in the area of haemophilia, but we've all had special training related to the disease. Ideally a patient enrolled in the programme can count on a continuing relationship with his care-givers over many years.'

'Sandra, explain this to me,' begged Lisa. 'I'm not sure I understand it all.'

Sandra launched into a rapid flood of Italian, and her sister-in-law begin to nod thoughtfully.

'It sounds like a very good idea,' she said slowly. 'And it covers much more than just stopping the bleeding, doesn't it?'

'A whole lot more,' agreed Richard crisply. 'And I must say, for anyone unfortunate enough to suffer the disease, Sydney's a pretty good place to live. There's an active haemophilia society and most large hospitals have some haemophiliacs on their books. If you could see your way clear to settling here rather than travelling constantly, I think you'd be doing the boy a favour.'

Lisa shrugged unhappily.

'Well, it's certainly what I want to do,' she said. 'Tony loves it here and he's made a lot of friends at school. And as for me, I want to be in a home of my own, not in hotels all the time. But Mario won't give an inch. He still wants us to go to Italy with him in July. Perhaps if you talked to him, Richard—'

Richard winced.

'Well, I'll certainly give it a try,' he agreed. 'But I can't help feeling that I'm the last person your husband is likely to listen to. All the same, enrolling Tony in the programme is probably a good start. At the very least, if he has another bleeding episode we'll have all his records on computer. That means we'll be able to swing into action much faster than last time. Now, have you got any questions, Lisa?'

'Yes. When can I bring Tony in?'

He smiled at her eagerness.

'My next haematology clinic is on Thursday morning,' he said. 'Sandra will show you where to go to make an appointment. And tell Tony to bring a book to read while he's waiting his turn. The waiting-room reading matter's fairly hopeless at the moment, unless he enjoys power-boat magazines.'

'He probably would,' retorted Lisa with a grimace. 'He was very jealous when he heard that Sandra had been out in your speedboat. His big ambition in life is to drive one himself.'

'Is it indeed?' asked Richard, rising to his feet. 'Well, if you'd like to get it organised, Sandra, I'd be happy to take you all out one Sunday and let him achieve his ambition. Just give me a ring at home and let me know when you're free.'

Sandra stared at him in surprise and pleasure. How kind of him, she thought. Somehow kindness wasn't a quality she had associated with Richard Daly up until that point.

'All right, I will,' she agreed, as he shepherded them both to the door.

'And don't forget our dinner on Saturday, will you?' he called after her.

It was a balmy summer evening when Richard came to take Sandra out to dinner. Night had just fallen like a dark blue curtain over the harbour and across on the North Shore the lights were winking brightly. A faint breeze stirred the frangipani bushes in the front garden, sending a heady, sweet perfume drifting on the air. Sandra stood leaning on the parapet of the terrace, dividing her attention between the dark waters of the harbour and the street where Richard's car should soon appear.

She was wearing a blue and silver knee-length dress with ruffled sleeves and a lightweight silver shawl. After ransacking both her own jewellery box and Lisa's, she had finally settled on simple pearl drop-earrings and a matching pearl and silver necklace with a tiny heart-shaped pendant. She knew she looked her best, but nervousness still made her feel fluttery inside. Even though her clothes came from a famous boutique in Milan, there were some commodities even a boutique couldn't supply—like confidence and vibrant sex appeal, thought Sandra mournfully. Right at this moment she would give half a year's pay to be a man-eating siren of a woman. Headlights flashed at the top of the driveway and she scuttled hastily inside so that she could look suitably surprised and languid when the doorbell rang.

But when the doorbell did ring and she saw Richard standing there she forgot to

116

look either languid or surprised. He was wearing a black dinner suit with a white shirt and a black bow-tie. His red-gold hair gleamed like a lion's mane and in his hand he carried a small, delicate corsage made from an orchid with a spray of asparagus fern. Sandra gave him an admiring smile.

'You look nice!' she told him impulsively. 'I don't think I've ever seen you in anything but a tatty old lab coat before, or casual clothes.'

'And you took utterly stunning!' he replied, stepping forward and kissing her lightly on the cheek.

The touch of his lips against her skin released an odd, bubbly feeling inside her and she breathed deeply to steady herself. The spicy scent of his aftershave lotion mingled with her own Chanel No 5 came surging up to meet her. She stood still, savouring the essence of the moment and feeling acutely aware of the powerful masculine figure that towered over her. Then her fingers hesitantly moved out to touch the orchid.

'Is that for me?' she asked.

'If you'd like it,' he agreed. 'Here, let me put it on.'

He pricked his finger as he was pinning

it in place and swore horribly, which made them both laugh. Picking up her shawl, Sandra walked lightly across to the living-room.

'I'll just tell Lisa we're off,' she said.

Lisa came out and exchanged friendly greetings with Richard, and a moment later they were on their way.

'You never did tell me where you wanted to have dinner,' remarked Richard as they climbed into the car. 'So I've booked a table at the opera house restaurant. But if you feel you've already spent far too much of your life there I can always ring up and cancel.'

'Oh, don't do that,' she replied. 'I love the place. It always looks so dramatic and beautiful against the water. I don't mind how often I go there.'

The opera house did look beautiful, like a huge, half-opened clam-shell against the dark blue background of the water. As they climbed the steps of the building Sandra stared appreciatively at the throngs of elegantly dressed people milling around on their way to concerts inside.

'Do you know what my pet fantasy is?' she asked.

'You'd like me to cover you with

whipped cream and lick it off slowly?' suggested Richard wickedly.

Sandra gave him a quelling glance.

'No. I'd like to be centre stage in the opera house, right in the limelight,' she continued firmly. 'Just once, to see what it feels like. But I don't suppose it will ever happen, especially since I can't even sing. Still, it would be nice to feel important for once.'

'What are you talking about?' demanded Richard in amazement. 'You *are* important. Very important. People's lives depend on you, you help to alleviate human pain and suffering. What could be more important than that?'

Sandra smiled spontaneously.

'Oh, you're good for me, Richard!' she exclaimed. 'I've been around performers for so long that I'd almost forgotten that other values existed. Mario, for instance, simply can't understand why I want to work in a hospital.'

'Mario, Mario!' he muttered in exasperation. 'I'm sick of hearing about Mario. It's you I want to find out about, Sandra, not him.'

They were nearing the entrance to the restaurant now, so Richard took her arm and piloted her through the door. Once inside, Sandra had a hazy impression of candle-lit tables, red tablecloths and their own shadowy reflections in the huge plate-glass windows that framed the night sky. A white-jacketed waiter led them to a table with a view of the harbour and soon produced Scotch on the rocks for Richard and a Cinzano amaro with ginger ale for Sandra. Then he handed them menus, whisked their napkins on to their laps with all the precision of a bullfighter flapping a cape and beat a smooth retreat.

'Now, tell me all about the real Sandra Calvi,' urged Richard, leaning forward and smiling at her. 'I want to know all about you—where you grew up, what sort of things you care passionately about. Everything that makes you special.'

He wasn't touching her, but he didn't need to. His tawny golden gaze lingered so warmly on her body that it was like an intimate caress. Sandra took a swift gulp of her drink and felt the bitter-sweet liquid fizz in her mouth and send a tingling current through her limbs.

'There's nothing much to tell,' she said hastily. 'I had a very happy childhood in Orvieto, which is a beautiful little town in the centre of Italy. It has a wonderful Gothic cathedral, a cake shop that sells incredibly delicious cakes and a ballet school where the lessons are held in a Palladian villa.'

'So you spent your early years stuffing yourself with cakes, prancing around in a tutu and going to church?' quizzed Richard.

'Something like that,' agreed Sandra. 'And then, when I was twelve, we migrated to Australia. The whole family, including Mario and Lisa. He was twenty-seven, and already married.'

He frowned thoughtfully.

'That's a big age gap,' he remarked. 'Fifteen years. Were there other children in the family?'

She looked down at her plate.

'No, but there was a reason for the gap. I was adopted,' she blurted out.

Richard's hand came out and covered hers. 'Is that a problem for you?' he asked sympathetically.

'No,' she said swiftly. 'The Calvis were wonderful parents to me, even though they were well into their forties when I was born. And in the circumstances I was very lucky that they took me on. Apparently

121

my real mother was only seventeen and unmarried—poor kid.'

'You've never tried to trace her?' asked Richard.

Sandra shook her head.

'No,' she replied. 'I thought it would only cause too much heartache for everyone concerned. And I've never had any problems in accepting the Calvis as my family. Although I must admit that it makes me feel doubly guilty about this rift with Mario, especially when he's done so much for me.'

Richard sighed impatiently. 'That's ridiculous!' he scoffed. 'You're just looking for an excuse to feel guilty.'

'No, I'm not!' she retorted hotly: 'How would you feel if you had a feud going on in your family?'

'I don't have a family!' he snapped.

They were still staring at each other fiercely when the waiter coughed discreetly at Richard's elbow.

'Are you ready to order yet, sir?' he asked in a bland voice.

'No, I'm afraid not,' replied Richard, instantly reverting to his usual courteous manner. 'Perhaps you could give us another five minutes?'

'Certainly, Sir,' agreed the waiter, melting into the background.

Sandra drew in her breath in a long, uneven sigh and then smiled frostily. She was determined not to let the evening degenerate into a shouting match.

'My God, if looks could kill, I'd be turning up my toes under the table right this minute,' remarked Richard to nobody in particular.

'Well, it's your fault,' she hissed. 'You started it!'

'Oh, no!' he protested, flinging up his hands in horror. 'I'm not going to be drawn into arguing the toss about that. If you want to hassle it out later in the evening, that's fine. We haven't had a decent row yet, and I must say I'm rather looking forward to it. But I'm damned if I'm going to sit in a public place while you look daggers at me all evening. So just put a proper smile on your face and behave yourself, Sandra. Is that clear?'

She glowered at him silently.

'Well, is it?' he insisted.

'Yes,' she said through her teeth.

'Good. Now the smile.'

She bared her teeth in such a ferocious grimace that Richard gave an explosive chuckle. After a moment Sandra's lips twitched reluctantly and she joined in his laughter.

'That's better,' he murmured, trailing one finger lightly across the back of her hand. 'Now let's get ready to order.'

They both perused their menus in silence for a moment, then Richard looked up with a puzzled frown.

'All right,' he said. 'You're the expert on everything Italian. What the hell is *bistecca alla pizzaiola?*'

Sandra glanced down at the menu.

'It's a prime cut of Florentine beefsteak, charcoal grilled, and smothered with a delicious, tangy sauce of fresh tomatoes, garlic, capers and basil,' she replied instantly.

'You really know your stuff!' exclaimed Richard. 'I'm impressed.'

'You shouldn't be,' she retorted pertly. 'I read it off the English translation on the other side of the menu!'

They both laughed, and after that the tension between them seemed to dissolve. Sandra ordered oysters Kilpatrick and Richard an entrée of wafer-thin honeydew melon with prawns. And, of course, they both had to try the famous *bistecca alla pizzaiola*. For several minutes they chatted lightly about everything from pathology tests to power-boat racing, but it was only when Sandra had finished her oysters that she returned to a subject which intrigued her. Swallowing the last delectable morsel with its hot sauce of bacon and Worcestershire sauce, she sat back and dabbed her lips with her napkin.

'Richard,' she said, 'there's something you mentioned before that puzzles me. You said you didn't have any family. But why not? What happened to them?'

He stared broodingly into his glass of chilled Riesling for a moment.

'Well, I wasn't a product of test-tube conception,' he retorted with a grim attempt at humour. 'But my family didn't last long. My father lit out when I was two years old and my mother was left to raise me on her own. She was a wonderful woman. I don't think I realised how wonderful until she died.'

'Died?' echoed Sandra.

Richard tossed off a large gulp of wine and grimaced.

'Yes,' he agreed flatly. 'She died of a perforated appendix when I was nine. I've always felt it was my fault.'

'What?' she demanded. 'How could it possibly be?'

A shadow passed over his face. 'Well, you, see,' he explained, 'she told me to come straight home after school one day because she wanted to buy me new shoes. I forgot all about it and went off to play football in the park with my mates. When I finally got home it was about five o'clock. I remember it all so vividly. We lived in a boarding house in London, on the very top floor, where you get a view of all the chimney-pots and the sky. It was nearly dark when I got home and you wouldn't believe how bleak and miserable London can be in February. I went running up the stairs, flight after flight of them, covered in torn linoleum, and there was a smell of stale curry in the air. And just as I set foot on the last flight of stairs I heard her. These dreadful, ear-splitting shrieks. I can't imagine why nobody had gone up to investigate. I tore up the last few stairs and flung open the door, but it was obvious that she was in a really bad way. I ran and called an ambulance, but she died an hour later in hospital.'

His hand tightened round the stem of

the wine glass until Sandra thought the fragile glass would snap. Reaching out, she gently prised his fingers loose and covered them with hers.

'And you thought it was your fault for being late?' she asked softly.

'Well, wasn't it?' he retorted savagely. 'If I'd done as she told me, I'd have been home nearly an hour earlier. That hour might have saved her life.'

Sandra squeezed his hand warmly.

'Oh, Richard,' she murmured, 'you were only a child, and children are heedless by nature. Do you mean you've been carrying around this terrible load of love and guilt for—what? Thirty years?'

'Twenty-nine,' muttered Richard hoarsely. 'Twenty-nine last Friday.' He was silent for a moment, staring down sightlessly at their joined hands. 'It made me feel so powerless,' he said at last. 'I kept thinking, "If only there were something I could have done."'

'Is that why you went into medicine?' asked Sandra shrewdly.

He gave her a startled look, as if the idea had never occurred to him.

'Yes, I suppose it was, ultimately,' he admitted. 'But don't run away with the idea that I made up my mind when I was nine that I was going to set out and save the world. Quite the reverse. I became completely uncontrollable.'

'What happened to you?' she asked sympathetically. 'Did you go to relatives?'

'No, there weren't any—at least, none that wanted me. I went into a Barnardo boys' home. They did their best for me, but I was pretty unpromising material. In the end they shipped me out to Australia, where I created total havoc around me.'

'So how did you get from being a wild teenager in a home to being a respected doctor in a posh suburb?' asked Sandra curiously.

Richard took another swift gulp of wine.

'I finally decided when I was about fifteen that there wasn't much point in taking out my grief and anger on the rest of the world,' he said carelessly. 'But I shouldn't be babbling on like this. I'm sorry. I don't usually talk about it, and I'm probably boring you senseless.'

'You're not boring me at all,' replied Sandra, but at that moment the *bistecca alla pizzaiola* arrived and Richard was saved from further conversation.

The steak was just as delicious as it

sounded, and came with a mound of sautéed potatoes with bacon and chopped parsley and an assortment of just-tender carrots and green beans. As she ate Sandra eyed Richard thoughtfully, assessing the new information he had given her. Yes, it fitted in. She had always felt that beneath his polished exterior there was a gritty determination that was not the product of an easy life. Yet somehow he touched her on the raw. Some instinct told her that he didn't often confide in people, and she was stirred by his willingness to share such painful memories with her.

'How are you finding the hospital routine?' he asked, obviously anxious to turn the conversation into more predictable channels.

'Fine,' she answered. 'It's busy, of course, but I like that. We've got one sister on each of the four-bedded wards, but there's some overlap with the enrolled nurses, because of the private wards. It would be good to have more staff, but we cope.'

'And you like the work?' prompted Richard.

'Yes, I do. It's mostly routine gynae stuff—women with hysterectomies, D &

Cs, ligation of Fallopian tubes, laparoscopic investigations, that sort of thing. My feet ache by the end of the day, but I really feel as if I'm doing something useful.'

'You're not missing the jet-setting life, then?' he quizzed.

'Not in the least,' said Sandra emphatically. 'I'm not really a jet-setter at heart.'

Richard smiled. 'That's becoming increasingly obvious,' he remarked drily. 'All the stylish clothes had me fooled at first, but I suspect now that you're just a plain ole homebody, deep down.'

'I don't know about "plain ole",' protested Sandra. 'But I have to admit that I'm one of the few human beings on this planet who really don't like travelling much. I go to see my mother in Italy each summer and that's nice, but apart from that my heart sinks at the mere thought of airports and jet lag and Customs and the whole rigmarole. My idea of pure heaven is lying under a tree in a hammock, reading a good book.'

'You're joking,' said Richard in an appalled voice. 'That would bore me rigid.'

'So what do you do for entertainment?' she challenged.

He shrugged. 'Fast cars, fast boats, fast women,' he summed up.

Sandra pulled a face. 'I can't help wondering what we're doing here together,' she muttered.

He flashed her his crooked smile. 'It's the attraction of opposites,' he said, drawing his forefinger down the inside of her wrist in a feather-light caress. 'It makes us irresistible to each other.'

'Oh, does it?' retorted Sandra sceptically, moving her arm.

'Well, anyway, you're enjoying Sydney, are you?' continued Richard, not in the least abashed.

'Yes,' she said with a satisfied sigh. 'Apart from anything else it's a tremendous relief not to have the responsibility for Tony any more. Oh, I shouldn't say that, should I? I forgot that you don't want to hear about my family.'

'No, no, tell me,' he urged reassuringly. 'Personally I think it was a very bad mistake for Mario to have you nursing Tony. I'd like to hear what you have to say on the subject.'

'Why do you think it was such a bad mistake?' asked Sandra with a frown. 'Don't you think I'm a good nurse?'

'Don't be ridiculous!' he snorted. 'From all I've heard at work, you're very competent. But that's not the point. It's a well-established principle in medical circles that doctors and nurses shouldn't treat their own close relatives—it's too hard to be objective about them. Besides, in your case, suppose Tony did have a serious accident and bled to death when you were in charge of him; wouldn't that exert an immense strain on family relationships?'

'I know!' agreed Sandra with feeling. 'Oh, Richard, you can't imagine how good it is to talk to somebody who understands that. It's always been my worst nightmare that he'd cut himself in some place where I just didn't have the facilities to deal with it. And Mario and Lisa don't seem to understand that I'm only a nurse, I'm not actually God. Mario in particular has this false sense of security when I'm there. But sometimes it's been awfully tough trying to deal with the poor kid, especially when we were abroad.'

'Tell me about it,' urged Richard.

'Well, in the first place,' she said, 'even hospital staff often don't know much about the treatment of haemophilia. I've had occasions right here in Sydney when I've had to go to Casualty with Tony and tell them how much cryo they need, where to get it, how to prepare it and how to give it. So you can just imagine trying to tackle all that in a foreign language. Apart from the disbelief that anything's actually wrong with the child, they usually ask me to produce a doctor's letter confirming that he's a haemophiliac, how severe the disability is and whether he has antibodies. And then the letter has to be translated, while all the time Tony lies bleeding furiously. I'm glad to be out of it, I can tell you! Anyway, Lisa and Tony and I all have other things that we want to do in our lives besides being Mario's support service. But I must say I'm really dreading his return.'

Richard sighed.

'Well, let's hope things improve now the kid's enrolled in our haemophilia programme,' he said. 'By the way, did you know we had a donation of another thousand pounds towards our coagulo-meter fund? If we get a good response to the revue and the other fund-raising activities, I'm hopeful we'll be able to buy it before the end of the year.'

For a while they chatted about fund-raising, and then there was the pleasant task of choosing puddings and lingering over coffee. After a creamy chocolate mousse, some strong black coffee and Belgian truffles, Sandra felt less inclined to worry about her brother's problems anyway.

'That was a delicious meal,' she murmured, smiling at Richard as they emerged from the restaurant. 'Thank you.'

'My pleasure,' he replied. 'Look, it's still fairly early and the weather's quite mild. Would you like to take a stroll along the waterfront?'

CHAPTER SEVEN

As they walked along the embankment towards the botanical gardens a faint sea breeze stirred Sandra's curls, blowing them back from her face. The moon was half hidden by a dark rack of cloud, but the lights from the city centre gleamed like coloured jewels across the water. And out in the darkness of the harbour there was all the colour and life of the water traffic. Red and green lights shone out

134

from passing boats and they heard the mournful, repeated hoot of a ship's whistle signalling the departure of some huge vessel. Richard put his arm casually around Sandra's shoulders. At the touch of his warm hand she stiffened momentarily, but then relaxed and even nestled into the curve of his arm. Leaning her head against him, she smiled.

'I can feel your heart beating,' she said aloud.

'And I can feel yours,' he retorted, stopping and swinging her into his arms. 'Right here. Fluttering like a frightened bird.'

Deliberately he laid his hand on her breast, cupping its roundness through the thin fabric. Her breath caught in her throat.

'You're not really frightened of me, are you, Sandra?' he asked huskily. And, putting his arms around her, he drew her to him. It was sheer delicious torment to feel his powerful male body thrust so intimately against her. His muscular thighs were spread apart, trapping her in his hold, and his breath fanned her cheek. She had to quell an urgent impulse to arch her back and raise her mouth to his.

'Not frightened,' she said uncertainly, 'but wary, perhaps. I don't know what to make of you. You seem so different from the things people say about you.'

'Oh? And what exactly do people say about me?' he demanded in a hard voice.

She hesitated and then gave in.

'That you're a womaniser,' she replied steadily. 'That you usually hang out with women who are incredibly glamorous and as hard as nails. Oh, Richard...it's not true, is it?'

'True enough,' he admitted with a sigh. 'But it's different with you, Sandra. I really feel something for you.'

She twisted angrily out of his grip and walked across to the sea wall.

'Oh, pull the other leg, Richard!' she snapped. 'I may be naïve, but I'm not that naïve! Do you use that line for all your conquests?'

He strode after her and gripped her by the shoulders, turning her to face him.

'You are not one of my conquests, damn it!' he shouted. 'And, apart from anything else, that's a bloody archaic way of looking at it! All right, I've had affairs with women, but they were always women who were old enough and experienced enough to know what they were doing, and I would hope that they got as much pleasure out of it as I did. It's a pretty normal human activity, for heaven's sake. And I'm thirty-eight years old! Was I supposed to live like a monk until you came along?'

Sandra gave a shaky sigh. It might be unreasonable, but she couldn't help being jealous of all those women who had shared Richard's bed.

'Didn't you ever think about getting married?' she flung at him.

'Yes, I thought about it!' he snapped. 'And I actually did it, too!'

She stared at him in horror.

'You're not—'

'No, I'm not married now,' he growled. 'I haven't been for years. The whole thing was a pitiful mistake anyway, and it only lasted a few months. I was twenty-seven at the time and just studying as a specialist in haematology. Karen was a North Shore socialite who ran a boutique and wanted a glamorous, status-symbol doctor to take around on her arm at parties like a Gucci handbag. She wasn't prepared for the reality of having me work eighty-hour weeks and, come home with clothes covered in blood from the operating theatre. She left me after six months and we were divorced three years later.'

'Do you still see her?' asked Sandra painfully.

'I couldn't even if I wanted to,' retorted Richard. 'She died of a malignant melanoma on the leg five years ago—too much sunbathing. It's ironical, really, when you consider how proud she was of her tan. I'm sorry she's dead, but I can't say I honestly feel any personal grief about it.'

'And ever since then there've only been casual affairs?' prompted Sandra.

'Yes,' said Richard shortly. 'Ever since then there've only been casual affairs. Karen made it pretty clear to me that I wasn't ideal husband material. She was probably right.'

Yet in spite of his careless shrug Sandra could hear the undertone of hurt pride in his voice. Reaching up, she touched his cheek.

'Did you love her?' she asked softly.

'Yes, I loved her!' he retorted. 'But it didn't do me much good, did it? According to her, I was married to my job and I was far too self-absorbed and insensitive to keep a wife happy. Well, that's one mistake I'll never make again. Marriage, I mean.'

Sandra was silent, feeling an obscure stab of dismay at this blunt statement. He looked down at her and gave a mirthless laugh.

'And how about you?' he demanded cruelly. 'What's a sweet, wholesome, old-fashioned girl like you doing on the shelf at the age of twenty-six? Particularly when she's so skilful at soothing men's fevered brows?'

She ignored the venom in his tone. She had seen too many patients in pain lash out at innocent bystanders to take it personally. Whatever unresolved suffering Richard's failed marriage had left him with, it wasn't her fault. Smiling ruefully at him, she wrinkled up her nose.

'I'm not sure I like that description!' she protested lightly. 'You make me sound like a cross between Florence Nightingale and Goody Two-Shoes.'

He let out his breath in a long, unsteady sigh, then his fingers played absentmindedly with her curls.

'Maybe you are,' he said with a touch of regret. 'But I'm sorry. I shouldn't make cheap shots like that just because I'm

139

disillusioned myself. All the same, it is a bit remarkable that you haven't married. You're very pretty and an unusually good listener, besides being loyal and capable. I'm surprised nobody has asked you.'

'I didn't say nobody had asked me!' replied Sandra with a touch of hauteur.

Richard grinned at her indignation.

'Ah, the plot thickens,' he murmured. 'So who was he? And why didn't you say yes? Did you think he'd turn out to be a wife-beater?'

Sandra gave a gurgle of laughter. Anybody less like a wife-beater than the mild, kindly Ken Jablonski was hard to imagine.

'No,' she said, resting her arms on the parapet and gazing out at the reflections on the water. 'He was a surgeon at a New York hospital. I went out with him for a couple of years, although my travelling interrupted things a lot. He was a very nice man.'

'Did you sleep with him?' asked Richard abruptly.

She felt her cheeks burn and was glad of the concealing darkness.

'I don't see that that's any of your business,' she said curtly.

'But did you?' he insisted.

She was silent for a moment and then let out a long, uneven sigh.

'No,' she admitted at last.

'Why not?' he asked.

'Because I didn't really want to,' she muttered. 'That's why I didn't marry him in the end. I thought if I was going to get married I probably ought to want to sleep with him or what was the point? Do you see what I mean?'

'I do indeed!' he replied in a strangled voice.

She flashed him a suspicious look. 'Are you laughing at me?' she demanded furiously.

His shoulders shook and a smothered guffaw escaped him. Seizing her by the shoulders, he drew her into his arms. She felt his entire body vibrate with silent laughter and stood rigid in his hold.

'I'm sorry,' he gasped, 'I can't help it, Sandra. You're so desperately earnest and so desperately innocent. It's rather touching, really.'

'Don't patronise me!' she retorted, nettled by his amusement. 'You may think it's funny, but I don't! All right, so I take relationships seriously and you

141

don't. But it doesn't really matter, does it? Because there's absolutely no need for us to see each other again after tonight!'

Richard's laughter died. 'Don't say that!' he begged. 'I want to see you again, Sandra.'

'Why?' she demanded suspiciously.

He sighed. 'Because I enjoy your company,' he said simply. 'All right, I'll come clean and admit that I'm very strongly attracted to you, but you don't have to take flight because of that, do you? It's not as though I'd force you to do anything you don't want. You can set the pace, but I do want to keep seeing you.'

His arms reached out, trapping her against the wall. But instead of trying to kiss her he simply buried his face in her hair and inhaled deeply as if he were trying to absorb her very essence. Sandra looked up at him with a tormented expression.

'What are you trying to say to me?' she demanded.

'Nothing too heavy,' he said, tracing a whorl on her cheek with his thumb. 'In some ways you're very young for your age, Sandra. Maybe it's because of your background. Lots of women of twenty-six would have already had half a dozen lovers and I'd have no qualms about making it clear that I wanted to be next on the list. But it's different with you.'

'Then what do you want from me?' she asked huskily.

His lips touched her hair, her throat, her mouth in a series of feather-light kisses.

'I want to get to know you,' he said. 'To spend time with you. To see you at work and to spend my evenings with you. I want you to give me a chance, Sandra.'

She looked at him doubtfully. All her usual common sense told her that she was playing with fire, that it would be pure madness to keep seeing Richard Daly. After all, hadn't he told her quite bluntly that he never intended to marry again and that casual affairs were all that he wanted? But his warm body was close to hers, she could smell the faint, primitive masculine odour of him, feel the thrilling hardness of his hand on her arm. A deep, pulsating heat began to throb through her and she realised that she was in the grip of a force that had nothing to do with common sense. She swallowed hard.

'Why don't you come to lunch tomorrow?' she asked. 'It's nothing special, just a casual family meal. But would you like to come?'

'A family meal?' he echoed, sounding rather taken aback. Then he saw the uncertainty in her eyes and smiled ruefully.

'Why not?' he agreed. 'It'll be a new experience for me.'

Then, drawing her into his arms, he kissed her with a tenderness that held only a hint of a more violent passion still to come.

Lunch at the Calvi's house the following day was a resounding success. Richard endeared himself to Lisa by hanging around in the kitchen nibbling morsels of cheese and salami and chatting casually while she prepared the main course. And he won Tony's heart by taking them all out in his speedboat during the afternoon and allowing the boy to take the wheel for a short time. Tony returned from the outing incoherent with bliss and ready to be Richard's devoted slave for life. By the end of the day Sandra felt comfortably certain that, however much Mario might resent her new admirer, the others loved him. It was a good beginning.

When she arrived at work on Monday

morning she felt as buoyant and excited as if she had just won a lottery. At first the day went well. From the time Sandra came on duty at seven a.m. there was never a quiet moment. First she was busy giving medications and injections and organising patients for breakfast. Then, after the visiting medical officers' rounds, she had to do chair-showers and mouth-toilets for some of her patients and inspect pressure areas on those who were confined to bed. After morning tea there were more medications, injections and observations to do, and she was returning from these when the duty sister called her into the office.

'Nurse Calvi,' she said, looking up from a pile of orders from the VMO rounds, 'I'm desperately busy checking these Pathology and X-ray requests. Can you do something for me? Nurse Greenlaw has just gone off sick with abdominal pain and she has a patient on Ward 364 called Mrs Jillian Roberts. Mrs Roberts had a D & C this morning after a spontaneous abortion and, although she's come through the operation well, she seems a bit weepy about losing the baby. Could you just pop in for five minutes and try to cheer her up?'

'Yes, of course,' agreed Sandra. 'May I see her file first?'

The file told her that Jillian Roberts was twenty-eight, had two living children and had suffered heavy bleeding at nine weeks of pregnancy followed by a spontaneous abortion. But that didn't quite prepare Sandra for the pathos of the slender, chestnut-haired woman who was sobbing into a wad of Kleenex when she tapped at the door of the ward. She gazed up sharply at Sandra's knock and made a small, futile attempt to stuff the tissues under her pillow.

'Sorry,' she said with a catch in her voice. 'I just can't seem to stop crying.'

'Don't apologise,' urged Sandra soothingly. 'Do you mind if I come in and talk? It might help if you had a chat about it.'

She plumped up Mrs Roberts's pillows behind her head and then sat down in the chair beside her bed.

'You must have wanted the baby very badly,' she murmured.

'Yes, I did,' agreed Mrs Roberts, biting her lip. 'I'd been trying to fall pregnant for over a year and then this had to happen. It seems so unfair.'

146

Sandra let her talk for a while about her disappointment over the miscarriage and the shock she had felt when it happened, then tried to lead her on to a more cheerful topic.

'You've already got a couple of children, though, haven't you?' she asked.

A watery smile lit Mrs Roberts's face.

'Yes,' she agreed, rummaging in the drawer of her bedside locker to produce a colour photo. 'Here they are. Emily and Amy. Emily's six and Amy's four.'

Two bright-eyed imps with pigtails smiled mischievously out of the photo at Sandra.

'They look gorgeous,' she said sincerely.

'Oh, they are,' agreed Mrs Roberts. 'They're such a joy to me. Jim's bringing them in tonight to visit me.'

'Well, we can't have you in tears when they come, can we?' asked Sandra. 'Is there anything I can get you that might brighten you up a bit? A magazine or something special to eat or drink?'

'I don't think so, thanks,' sighed Mrs Roberts, leaning back against the pillows with an exhausted expression. 'I'm not normally the weepy type, you know, but somehow all this seems to have got on

147

top of me. I might have a sleep, actually. I don't seem to have any energy at all right now.'

'Well, don't let it worry you,' said Sandra comfortingly. 'It's just the after-effects of the op. In another day or two you'll probably be as fit as a flea.'

But that was just where she was wrong. In the nature of Richard's work he spent most of his time in the haematology laboratory and was rarely seen on the wards. Yet the following afternoon he appeared with a folder of documents and spent ten minutes closeted in the senior sister's office. Sandra was passing by as he emerged and stopped, hoping to exchange a word or two with him, but he didn't even appear to see her. Looking back into the office, he spoke through gritted teeth.

'Well, you'd better phone Mr Roberts right away, please, Sister,' he said. 'Dr Steptoe wants to break it to them together. The sooner we start treatment with something like this, the better.'

She went on her way with a sinking feeling in the pit of her stomach. Whatever was wrong with Mrs Roberts, it was obviously something more than just the after-effects of a D & C. But it was not until the following morning that she found out exactly what it was. Sister Fleming called her into her office and delivered the news abruptly.

'Two things, Nurse Calvi. Janet Greenlaw has had an operation for appendicitis, so we'll have a relief nurse working on the wards from this afternoon onwards. And there's one of Nurse Greenlaw's patients that I'd like you to take over. It's Mrs Roberts. She's just been diagnosed as suffering from acute myeloid leukaemia, and Dr Steptoe, the oncologist, wants her to begin chemotherapy as soon as possible. Mrs Roberts particularly mentioned that she'd like you to nurse her. Apparently she has found you very considerate and helpful.'

Sandra was touched by the compliment, but at the same time she was dismayed at the severity of the diagnosis. For the rest of the day her thoughts kept straying back to the leukaemia patient, and she was still feeling depressed when she emerged into the car park that afternoon. To her surprise Richard hailed her from the steps of the haematology building.

'Hello, Sandra,' he called. 'Are you coming to the revue rehearsal tonight?'

She pulled a comic face.

'Yes, I am,' she agreed. 'Barry's been twisting my arm, and in a fit of madness I've not only agreed to play the part of the TV reporter, but I'm also handling props as well. Most of the equipment is available from the hospital, but, if you happen to know anybody who has an antique brass microscope circa 1880, tell them I'll crawl on my hands and knees if they'll lend it to me.'

Richard looked amused.

'Is that a promise?' he demanded. 'Because I've got one in my study at home. I picked it up at an antique sale once as a curiosity—'

'Really?' she said. 'But would you be prepared to lend it?'

'Sure,' he agreed. 'I know you'll take care of it. And it's pretty robust anyway. Do you want to come and see it?'

'When?' she asked.

'Now, if you like. It's about time I knocked off; I've been here since six-thirty this morning. Come back to my place and I'll make you some coffee.'

Half an hour later they were sitting on the terrace, at Richard's house, looking out over the blue waters of the harbour. The brass microscope was carefully packed in a wooden box at Sandra's feet, but after her first transports of joy at seeing it she had lapsed back into the depression that had dogged her all day.

'What's the matter?' asked Richard, pouring her more coffee. 'You look awfully miserable.'

She shrugged and forced a smile. 'Difficulty in switching off,' she replied. 'You know how it is. Some patients just seem to prey on your mind.'

'Oh, I see,' he agreed soberly. 'Who is it? Jilly Roberts?'

'How did you know?' she asked in a startled voice.

'It had to be, didn't it?' he replied. 'She's the only person you're nursing at the moment who has a life threatening illness. And she's young, with little kids depending on her. It's bound to be a bit of a kick in the teeth for everybody involved. I felt the same way myself when I saw the results of the tests and examined her. Red-cell production down, platelet-production down, normal white blood cells down, abnormal white blood cells up—all the classic symptoms. And if she hadn't come in with that miscarriage probably nobody

151

would have even suspected until it was too late.'

Sandra winced. 'Oh, don't,' she begged. 'It makes me cringe when I think of the way I was rabbiting on to her yesterday, telling her she'd be fine again in a few days.'

'Well, it will take more than a few days,' said Richard grimly. 'But with a bit of luck she'll be fine. She's in for a rough time, of course, with the chemotherapy and irradiation for the enlarged spleen, but I think she'll pull through. She has a very strong will to live and everybody on the staff will be fighting for her. Now, with all that said, you've somehow got to detach yourself from it, Sandra.'

'I suppose you're right,' she muttered.

Richard put his fingers under her chin and lifted her face to his.

'I know I'm right,' he insisted firmly. 'But if it's any comfort to you there's another really good reason why Jilly Roberts is likely to survive.'

'Oh? What's that?' asked Sandra.

'Her family is one hundred per cent behind her. Her husband was devastated by the diagnosis, but he's determined that she's going to survive. And, of course, she's desperately anxious to live for his sake and for the children. That kind of commitment really inspires me.'

'I thought you weren't into commitment,' pointed out Sandra with a hint of tartness.

He sighed.

'As far as my private life goes, I suppose I'm not,' he admitted reluctantly. 'But as a doctor I must say that sometimes it's the one and only thing that keeps people going.'

A remark that made her wonder whether Richard was quite as heartless and insensitive as she had first thought.

CHAPTER EIGHT

In the days that followed Sandra saw a good deal of Richard on the ward. Because of the severity of Jilly Roberts's illness chemotherapy had to start immediately, and this meant that reverse barrier nursing was needed. It was often hard for patients' families to accept the need for this and, after the oncologist had explained it all to the Robertses, Richard and Sandra found themselves drawn into another informal conference with the couple. On the day before Jilly Roberts's treatment was due to begin Richard called Sandra into the ward.

Pushing open the door, she entered the room and saw that Richard and a tall man with a greying brown beard and wild curly hair were standing on either side of the bed. Propped against the pillows was the patient, wearing a green and white broderie anglaise nightdress with a matching négligé.

'Sandra, you've met Mr Roberts, haven't you?' asked Richard.

'Yes,' agreed Sandra. 'Hello, Mr Roberts. How are you?'

'Still reeling from the shock, to put it bluntly,' he replied. 'That's why I wondered if you and Mr Daly could have a little talk with us just to set a few things straight. Dr Steptoe the cancer specialist already had a word to us about this chemotherapy and...what do you call it? Barrier nursing?'

'Yes,' nodded Sandra. 'Actually it's reverse barrier nursing in this sort of case. Barrier nursing is when you keep

154

the patient isolated in order to protect other people. When the isolation is meant to protect the patient, it's called reverse barrier nursing.'

Jim Roberts looked baffled. 'Well, anyway,' he continued, 'what Dr Steptoe said was a bit over our heads, so we thought we'd ask you and Dr Daly to clear it up for us. Dr Daly's been real helpful already, and Jilly reckons she'll get on well with you. Anyway, we'd just like to ask you a few questions.'

'Yes, of course,' agreed Sandra. She settled herself comfortably in a chair and smiled at Jilly.

'Do you like my nightdress, Nurse Calvi?' asked Jilly. 'Jim bought it for me as a present. He said if I was going to lie around in bed for weeks on end I might as well took glamorous while I was at it.'

'It's lovely,' said Sandra.

'Now, what would you like to know first?' asked Richard.

'Well, leukaemia,' muttered Jim with an uneasy sideways glance at his wife. 'Isn't that usually fatal?'

'Not these days,' replied Richard crisply. 'There's a lot of unnecessary fear about leukaemia, you know. In the past it was often a death sentence, but that simply isn't the case any more. It's still a serious illness, but with chemotherapy there's every chance that you'll make a complete recovery, Mrs Roberts.'

'Jilly,' murmured the patient huskily.

'All right—Jilly. But the chemotherapy does have a few disadvantages, and we wouldn't be playing fair if we hid those from you. The main problem is that it seriously depresses your immune system and your ability to fight off infection. Consequently we have to keep you isolated while you're having the treatment. That's where the reverse barrier nursing comes in. What it means in practice is that we'll keep you in a ward with glass windows and limit your visitors. Anyone who comes into the ward will have to wear a mask and gown, and it will be very important to keep people away if they have any infection, no matter how minor. Even a common cold could be very dangerous to you. Now I know this is going to be very hard on you, especially since your little girls are really too young to understand the need for it. But you'll just have to remember that it's only for a limited time. There's every chance that you'll make a complete recovery and be back home with your family very soon.'

'I certainly will if I have anything to do with it!' retorted Jilly firmly.

'Good for you,' applauded Richard. 'Now, is there anything else you want to ask either of us?'

'Well,' said Jilly with less certainty, 'you mentioned that the chemotherapy had several disadvantages. What are the others?'

'Sandra—over to you,' urged Richard.

Sandra marshalled her thoughts carefully before she spoke. She didn't want to distress her patient any further.

'Increased tendency to bleed,' she said. 'But there are various things we can do to cope with that, like padding the bed-rails. Unfortunately there's likely to be some nausea and vomiting but, again, there are drugs that can be used to help that. Possibly some anaemia, which can make you feel very tired and which may need blood transfusions—'

'Will there be a lot of pain?' broke in Jilly anxiously.

'There may be some pain,' admitted Sandra. 'But patients usually cope well with the right drugs.'

'Will my hair fall out?' asked Jilly.

'Yes,' replied Richard. 'But the side-effects of the chemotherapy will really only become obvious after a couple of weeks when bone-marrow suppression occurs. And the hair loss is only temporary. Your hair will grow back when the treatment ends. And you can get a wig in the meantime.'

Jilly caught her breath and her fingers travelled anxiously up to her thick chestnut locks. For a moment her self-control wavered dangerously and she bit her lip.

'How about a blonde wig?' suggested Sandra hastily. 'You'd look terrific as a blonde.'

Jilly gave a long, shuddering sigh. 'Yes, I would, wouldn't I?' she agreed with barely a tremor in her voice. 'How would you fancy me as a blonde, Jim?'

'I'd fancy you any way at all, love,' replied Jim, crushing her fingers in his.

'Well, you've both got the right attitude,' said Richard approvingly. 'And that's what counts most. In many ways the worst thing you'll have to deal with in the next few weeks or months is the emotional stress of all this—feelings of anxiety, irrational guilt, fear, not knowing what's going on.

And the way to handle that is to ask for help. We're always happy to explain the hospital procedures to you, and if you want to see someone like a priest or a cancer counsellor we can arrange that for you too. What we want to do is provide the best possible environment for you to get well again. And I'm sure you will. Now is there anything else you want to ask?'

The couple exchanged glances and shook their heads in unison.

'Then we'll leave you alone together,' said Richard gently, shepherding Sandra to the door. 'But remember, if there's ever anything I can do, just call me. Day or night, it doesn't matter.'

'Thanks, Doc,' replied Jim, stretching out his hand. 'You've been great. You too, Nurse.'

Together Sandra and Richard walked down the corridor to her nursing station.

'Well, I'd better get back to the lab,' said Richard with a sigh. 'I've got some Factor assays to do and heaps of paperwork. Oh, and by the way, the TV station rang me up this morning and they'd like to film that programme about blood donors tomorrow morning. Will that suit you?'

'Yes, that's fine,' agreed Sandra. 'Now

where do I have to go and how do I get there?'

'I'll drive you,' he said. 'I'll pick you up from your place about nine o'clock.'

It was shortly after nine-thirty when they arrived at the blood transfusion centre the following morning. A grey-haired woman with glasses and a pleasant face came forward to meet them, accompanied by a burly man in blue overalls.

'Hello, Dr Daly,' she said. 'I've spoken to you on the phone, but I don't think we've met before. I'm Sister in charge of the centre and my name is Jean Ray. And you must be Sandra Calvi.'

'Yes,' agreed Sandra, smiling.

'And this is our guinea-pig, Ted Lewis,' added Sister Ray. 'Ted's an old hand who's been on our books for years, so we actually have all his records on file here. But I believe that, for the sake of the cameraman, you want to go through all the usual drill with the blood-transfusion form, Dr Daly. Is that right?'

'Yes,' agreed Richard. 'I'm expecting the camera crew to arrive any time now, so we'd better get set up for them.'

'We've screened a cubicle at the far end for you,' said Sister Ray. 'And if you just call me when you're ready I'll come and take the blood. Nurse Calvi can sit and chat to Ted about the football. He'll enjoy that, won't you, Ted?'

'Too right I will,' agreed Ted with an admiring glance at Sandra.

Ten minutes later they were ready to start. There was a brief introductory outline of the programme from the reporter Charles Beveridge, then the cameras swung across to Richard. He spoke eloquently about the vital work done by the Red Cross and the need for more blood donors. After a few questions from the reporter, which Richard handled smoothly, they switched across to Sandra. She sat, outwardly relaxed but inwardly nervous, at a table while the video cameraman circled around to get the best possible shot of her.

'Now, tell me, Doctor,' said Charles, 'aren't there a lot of risks associated with giving and receiving blood these days, especially with the AIDS virus and diseases like hepatitis being spread by blood products?'

'The risks are very small,' replied Richard soothingly. 'And all donors are very carefully screened, as you'll realise if you see the forms they're asked to fill in before donating blood.'

With a swift nod from the video operator, Sandra found herself suddenly on camera. After a moment's panic she relaxed and smiled warmly at the blood donor.

'Good morning, Mr Lewis,' she said. 'I understand you want to make a blood donation, but before we can take blood from you we need to find out some details about your health. If you can fill in this form for us, then we'll go ahead. I'll run through the questions with you, and if you need any help just stop me. Now, have you ever given blood before? Have you ever had any of the following—diabetes, kidney disease, rheumatic fever, chest trouble, bleeding disorders, asthma—?'

As she rattled off the list of illnesses, Sandra glanced up at Richard and received a reassuring wink. She felt confidence flowing through her and she was able to deal as easily and naturally with the blood donor as if there were no cameraman or reporter in the room. Once she had completed the list of questions about dental work, vaccinations, blood transfusions, tattoos, malaria and other details, she produced a copy of the declaration relating to AIDS.

'Now, I'll just get you to read through this and sign it if you feel satisfied that you're not at risk,' she said. 'And after that one of the Red Cross nurses will come and take some blood from you.'

Mr Lewis read through the forms with his lips moving and then signed them with a flourish of his massive red hand.

'There you go,' he said triumphantly.

Sister Ray asked Mr Lewis to lie down and then used a blood-pressure cuff to pump up the vein in his arm before inserting a cannula. As the blood flowed out into the bag Sandra kept an eye on the flow and chatted casually to the man, who was lying stoically on the couch. Shortly after, the cameraman filmed a close-up shot of a smiling Sandra offering Mr Lewis a large chocolate milk shake and then her part was over. With a sigh of relief she withdrew to a corner of the room to watch Richard. Charles Beveridge asked some questions about the next step in the handling of donated blood, then filming stopped.

'Good stuff,' said Charles approvingly as they left the building together. 'Now we'll ride over with the refrigerated van as it delivers blood to the Nelson Hospital and we'll catch up with you two about eleven o'clock. Then we can film the last section, showing how you actually make use of the blood in hospital. And if you have a genuine patient who's having a transfusion and is prepared to be shown on television, all the better. If anything can make people understand how valuable their blood donations really are, that will do it.'

As he held the car door open for Sandra. Richard touched her affectionately on the arm.

'Thanks, Sandra,' he said. 'You did a really good job. Let's hope the last part goes as well.'

'Have you got any patients who are prepared to be filmed?' she asked.

'Yes,' he replied sombrely. 'Jilly Roberts has volunteered. Dr Steptoe wants her to have a blood transfusion anyway for anaemia, and I was telling her about the programme. She offered right away to be part of it. She said that if her illness could do some good to other people, then she wouldn't feel so depressed about it.'

'That's brave of her,' murmured Sandra.

'Yes, isn't it? And that same bravery will help her overcome the cancer, so don't start looking upset about it.'

His lean brown fingers came off the steering-wheel for a moment and covered hers.

'All right,' promised Sandra, 'I won't.'

Just the same, she found it very moving to stand gowned and masked in Jilly's isolation ward, administering the blood transfusion, while the cameraman filmed them both through the glass wall. Afterwards Jilly gave her a wry smile.

'Well, that's one of my ambitions fulfilled!' she said. 'I always wanted to be a TV star!'

'I'm glad that's over,' confided Sandra to Richard as the TV crew drove away much later. 'I didn't know I was going to find it so harrowing.'

'But worthwhile,' he reminded her. 'That programme will almost certainly send blood donations sky-rocketing, and that means lives will be saved. It's worth putting yourself through anything for that.'

She made a determined effort to be cheerful.

'Even wearing fluorescent green underpants and doing a belly-dance on stage?' she challenged.

'Even that,' he agreed with a pained

expression. 'Although I doubt if I could ever do it with the same pizzazz that Barry Ripper shows. He's probably our most successful fund-raiser yet.'

'How's the fund for the coagulometer coming along anyway?' asked Sandra curiously.

'Not too badly at all,' he said in a satisfied voice. 'We've got well over twenty thousand now, and there's still the hospital ball and a gala charity dinner coming up later in the year after the drama revue, not to mention a more down-market family barbecue next month. Would you like to come to that, by the way?'

She smiled. 'You still want to keep seeing me, then?' she asked.

'Every spare moment,' vowed Richard.

The next few weeks passed in a happy whirl of activity for Sandra. Although Richard worked long hours he was true to his promise and he did spend every spare moment with her. To their delight, the programme on blood transfusion brought an immediate response from viewers, and blood donations jumped dramatically. Yet it wasn't only work that Richard and Sandra shared. They went boating on the harbour, sometimes accompanied by an ecstatic Tony, who was allowed to drive the speedboat, they watched films and went to night-clubs and swam in the surf at Bondi Beach. They spent hilarious evenings rehearsing the hospital revue and five even more hilarious evenings performing it. They gloated together over the additional three thousand dollars in the fund for the coagulometer and they hatched plans for newer and more grandiose fund-raising efforts. And when the fine autumn weather broke up and chilly rain lashed the harbour they sat snug and warm in front of a blazing fire in Richard's living-room, chatting fitfully about medicine, Italian food and the meaning of life.

It would have been an idyllic time if there had not been a couple of nagging worries to cloud Sandra's happiness. Her first problem was that Richard still fought shy of any genuine involvement. On one occasion he told her that he couldn't see her at the weekend, 'because I'm staying at the Hamiltons' holiday house.' He didn't offer her any more explanation than that, and Sandra was too proud to press him. But that Saturday night she lay awake for hours, brooding over it and wondering about the exact nature of Richard's relationship with Felicity Hamilton. She was miserably aware that she was falling more and more deeply in love with Richard, but it seemed to be a process that she was powerless to halt. Rather like being drawn inexorably towards Niagara Falls, she thought grimly, while trying feebly to swim against the current.

Her other worry, which loomed larger as each day went by, was the forthcoming return of her brother Mario. Sandra had spoken to him on the telephone several times and he remained doggedly determined to undo all the changes she had made in her life. Once he got back, he promised, he would soon persuade her to give up that useless hospital job. What was even worse, he announced his intention, 'to sort out that swine Richard Daly.' Sandra had the sinking feeling that a battle of nuclear proportions was brewing.

The one place where she was able to shake off these private worries was at the hospital. After several weeks in the job she now felt completely confident and professional in her work. She was conscious of being a useful, highly valued member of a team, doing a difficult job and doing it well. Although there was occasional sadness involved this was far outweighed by the joy of seeing most patients recover. By Easter-time even her favourite patient, Jilly Roberts, was showing a good response to chemotherapy.

On Easter Sunday the two little Roberts girls came in to visit their mother, proudly bearing a basket of chocolate eggs and hand-painted cards. Because one of them had a slight cold they could not be allowed into the ward with their mother, but had to stand near the glass outside and hold up their cards for her to see. Sandra felt a lump rise in her throat as she saw Emily waving a large cardboard cut-out of the Easter bunny carrying a sign that said, 'GET WELL SOON MUMY'. Amy's card was even more pathetic—a mass of scribbles with a straggling row of kisses at the bottom. But when it was time to go home the trouble started. Amy's lower lip began to quiver dangerously and tears filled her eyes.

'I want to kiss my mummy goodbye,' she complained. 'Why can't I?'

'Oh, cripes,' muttered Jim Roberts, going on his knees beside the child. 'I explained all that to you, mate.'

Sandra stepped in hastily.

'Emily and Amy,' she said, 'did you know the Easter bunny left something for you in my office? Would you like to come and see what it is?'

Luckily she had a few chocolate eggs on hand for just such an emergency and the crisis was averted. But when she went in to check Jilly's temperature and pulse shortly afterwards she found the young woman sobbing desperately.

'Sometimes I can't bear it—I just can't bear it,' she gulped. 'I don't know if I'll ever get better.'

'Of course you will,' urged Sandra. 'You'll be back home with them before you know it.'

It was a conversation that would haunt her later.

A week after Easter Mario phoned to say that he was returning to Sydney the following day. It was Lisa who broke the news to Sandra and Richard. They were sitting on the floor of the Calvi's living-room playing Monopoly with Tony when the telephone rang. Lisa went out of the room to answer it and reappeared ten minutes later with a rueful expression.

'Richard,' she said, 'would you mind if I ask you not to come to dinner tomorrow night after all?'

Sandra had fallen into the habit of inviting Richard to join the family for casual meals at least once a week. By now it was almost a ritual.

'No, of course not,' he agreed swiftly. 'But is anything wrong, Lisa? You look a bit worried.'

'No, nothing's wrong,' replied Lisa with a meaningful glance at Tony. 'It's just that Mario's coming home tomorrow, which is wonderful news, isn't it, Tony? But he still feels the same way about several issues as he did before. And somehow I think he might need to get over his jet lag before he enjoys the pleasure of your company, Richard.'

Richard's tawny eyes glinted mischievously.

'You'll have to risk it sooner or later, Lisa,' he challenged.

Lisa winced. 'Why don't you come to dinner on Saturday, then?' she said in a failing voice. 'That will give me time to have a little chat to Mario first.'

'All right,' agreed Richard, gritting his teeth. 'But I think you'd better come back to my place for a drink now, Sandra. I have the feeling that we need a little chat on the subject too.'

Rather reluctantly Sandra allowed him to pull her to her feet. She had been feeling pleasantly cosy, lying in the firelight with nothing more urgent on her mind than how to win large chunks of Mayfair from Tony. Now she was being jolted back unpleasantly into the real world.

'All right,' she said crossly. 'But I'm not staying long—I have a headache.'

Once they reached Richard's house he led her into the living-room, poured a Campari and soda for her and lit the fire. Then he stood leaning against the mantelpiece, watching her with a searching expression.

'Well, what do you want to say?' she demanded.

'Just this. Mario can't stand the sight of me, and there's a real lulu of a battle brewing unless we do something to prevent it.'

'What can we do?' asked Sandra impatiently.

'You could move in here,' said Richard.

The bluntness of it took her breath away. She sat staring at him for a moment, then took a hasty gulp of her drink.

'If you think that would prevent a quarrel, then you obviously don't know my dear brother!' she exclaimed with a mirthless laugh. 'Sorry, Richard. I only feel strong enough for serious suggestions.'

'It *is* a serious suggestion,' he replied impassively.

'What?' She looked at him through narrowed blue eyes. 'You really want me to move in here?'

'Yes,' he agreed curtly.

'On what basis?' she asked.

He crossed the floor and crouched on the rug at her feet. He stared at her intently with his golden lion's eyes, then drew one finger slowly down her cheek.

'I've already had one failed marriage,' he said slowly, and I'm not keen to rush into a second one, as much for your sake as for mine. I think we ought to be very sure before we contemplate anything as serious as that. But isn't this the best way to find out? You know perfectly well that I want you, Sandra, I ache with wanting you. But I'm not going to rush you into any lovemaking that you're not ready for. All I'm saying is this. Share my life for a while, give us both a chance to find out how serious this relationship is. Does that make sense?'

Sandra was silent, acutely conscious of the ticking of a grandfather clock against the far wall, of the hiss and crackle of the flames in the fireplace, of her own tumultuously beating heart. She didn't want Richard to say that he wasn't keen to rush into marriage with her, that he needed time to find out how serious the relationship was. She wanted him to sweep her off her feet and smother her with kisses and beg her to be his wife. She wanted him to say that he loved her. But a drab inner voice told her that there weren't going to be any guarantees, just a gamble that might or might not work out. He was scrutinising her closely, waiting for her answer with a searing intensity in his eyes.

'Maybe it does,' she said bleakly. 'But I can't make a decision about it tonight. There's too much involved. And I really do have a headache, Richard.'

'All right,' he said, rising to his feet with a sigh. 'But will you at least think about it and perhaps give me an answer when I come to dinner on Saturday?'

'I'll think about it,' was all that Sandra would promise.

The dinner was an utter disaster. Sandra's headache had been succeeded by a bad cold, Tony was showing off outrageously and Mario and Richard were glaring at each other with barely concealed antagonism throughout the meal. Lisa did her best to keep things going well, but her efforts were doomed. Even the delicious chicken and egg soup, the main course of veal with tomato, basil and fried potatoes and the home-made cassata ice-cream were not enough to keep Mario's mind off his pet theme. Wiping his mouth with his napkin as he finished eating, he raised his glass of chilled Soave wine.

'*Brava*, Lisa,' he complimented his wife. 'Your cooking is as good as ever. And you'll have plenty of time to collect more recipes in Milan this summer. What do you say to three months in Italy, eh, Tony?'

He pinched his son's cheek, but Tony slouched sulkily away from his touch.

'I don't want to go to Italy!' he said defiantly. 'I like it here!'

'Don't be ridiculous, boy!' snapped Mario. 'You know we always go to Italy for the summer. Your mamma's looking forward to it.'

175

'No, I'm not,' said Lisa flatly. 'I don't want to go either.'

There was a moment's hushed silence. Then Mario turned his burning gaze on Sandra.

'This is all your fault!' he accused. 'You've turned my wife and child against me!'

'That's not true!' retorted Sandra hotly. 'I had nothing to do with—'

But before she could finish her sentence she was attacked by a fit of sneezing. Groping for a box of tissues, she glared at Mario with streaming eyes.

'Leave me alone!' she said in a muffled voice. 'Can't you see I've picked up an awful cold at the hospital? I don't feel well enough to argue!'

'Ha!' cried Mario. Well, you wouldn't catch colds if you stayed home and looked after Tony, would you?'

'Don't be so utterly ridiculous!' she stormed.

It was at this point that Richard intervened. Rising to his feet, he stood staring contemptuously at Mario.

'Stop bullying her!' he said sharply. 'Can't you see she's not feeling well? Look, Lisa, thanks for the meal, but I think it's a total waste of time to try and discuss anything right now. Sandra and I had better be going.'

'Going?' echoed Sandra in a startled voice.

'Yes,' said Richard, taking her hand and pulling her to her feet. 'Come back to my place and I'll make you a whisky and hot lemon.'

'Over my dead body!' growled Mario, leaping to his feet and moving to block the doorway. 'If you leave this house with that man, Sandra, you needn't bother coming back.'

Richard stepped forward with his square jaw jutting threateningly out.

'Well, you needn't think that's going to stop her!' he said. 'She was planning to come and live with me anyway.'

'Is this true, Sandra?' demanded Mario in horror.

Sandra opened her mouth to protest, then stopped with an appalled expression on her face. Whatever she said now, it was going to be totally disastrous. Events were moving too fast and she felt as if she were being swept along by some wild current that would dash her to pieces on hidden rocks. And yet, at the same time, she felt very calm and lucid. Four of the people she cared about most were staring at her, waiting for her decision, and all of them were reacting differently. Lisa looked dismayed, Tony enthralled, Mario furious, and Richard... She could not fathom the expression on Richard's face. There was a certain irritating brashness about it, and yet, beneath that, she glimpsed something far more profound—a look of fierce, urgent expectation. A muscle twitched in his temple and he held out his hand to her.

'You'll have to make a choice sooner or later, Sandra,' he said quietly. 'You'll have to decide whether you can trust me.'

Suddenly the rest of the room seemed to vanish, along with the onlookers. A bitter-sweet yearning filled Sandra's heart as she stared into his tawny eyes. Then slowly, as if in a dream, she moved towards him and put her hand in his.

'I do, Richard,' she murmured. 'And I'm coming with you.'

Richard could hardly conceal his smug look of triumph as he led her towards the door, and Mario flashed both of them an angry glare.

'You'll regret this, Sandra!' he warned, stabbing the air with his forefinger. 'He won't marry you! And it won't be long before he's playing around with other women either. He only wants to use you and cast you aside, so don't come running to me for pity when it happens!'

CHAPTER NINE

It felt strange to be living at Richard's house. For the first couple of days Sandra felt too sick and feverish with her cold to do much except lie in bed. She could not help resenting the devious way that Richard had propelled her into taking action. Yet he was so thoughtful and considerate about looking after her that she could not stay angry for long. Luckily she was rostered for a four-day break from work, which gave her time to recuperate. But for Richard it was business as usual. He was out of the house every morning by seven and he seldom returned home before seven o'clock at night. When he did arrive he liked to spend an hour or so after dinner chatting with her, usually about the day's events at the hospital.

But by common consent there was one subject they avoided at first—her rift with her brother.

Yet it was Richard who forced her to come to terms with the issue at last. On the fourth day after her arrival he came home unusually early and spent a long time out on the terrace alone, gripping the balustrade and staring out over the wind-whipped harbour. When at last he came inside he looked grim-faced and exhausted. Later, while he was kneeling on the hearth-rug, lighting the fire, he suddenly looked up at her as she sat sipping a glass of tawny port.

'Don't you think it's time you faced up to moving your belongings, if you're going to stay here?' he demanded abruptly.

Sandra winced. Up until now she had been managing with a suitcase full of clothes dropped in by a furtive-looking Lisa the day after her dramatic departure.

'I suppose so,' she admitted reluctantly.

Richard flung the lighted match into the fire and the pile of dry kindling and newspaper flared up with a sudden orange glow. Still half crouching, he crossed the floor and knelt on the Persian carpet in front of Sandra, so that his face was on a level with hers. Seizing her glass, he set it down firmly on a side-table and took her hands in his.

'I didn't want to force the issue before,' he said. 'Because I knew you weren't feeling well. But you're on the mend now, Sandra, and it's time you did something decisive one way or the other. Do you want to stay on here or not?'

Her throat ached with suppressed emotion.

'Do you want me to stay?' she demanded in a choking voice.

Richard gave an exasperated sigh.

'Do you even need to ask that?' he retorted fiercely. 'For heaven's sake, Sandra, I thought I'd made it clear how I felt about you. Of course I want you to stay! You can't imagine how good it feels to wake up in the morning and know that you're here and to look forward to seeing you when I come home at night. I only wish you'd stay on permanently.'

She was silent for a moment, then she drew in a long, ragged breath.

'All right,' she said.

'Good girl!' he cried exultantly, jumping to his feet. 'Will you phone Mario and ask for your things or shall I?'

'I'll do it,' she replied.

Yet her footsteps were leaden as she crossed the floor to the telephone and her fingers shook as she punched in the numbers. It was not an easy conversation and, after less than a minute, she heard the receiver at the other end crash down.

'Well?' prompted Richard.

Swallowing hard, she set down the receiver. 'He said he'll have my boxes delivered tomorrow,' she told him steadily.

By the time she went back to work, a couple of days later, she was feeling far more buoyant about her quarrel with Mario and her uneasy relationship with Richard. With returning good health her spirits rose. Something was bound to work out, she told herself. Richard would decide that he wasn't frightened of commitment, after all, and—by some unspecified miracle—the two men would become good friends.

'You're looking cheerful,' Sister Fleming greeted her as she reported for duty. 'Have you recovered from your cold, then?'

'Yes, thank you,' replied Sandra brightly. 'But it might be best if somebody else could nurse Jilly Roberts for a day or two just in case I'm still infectious.'

'Oh, my dear!' said Sister Fleming.

'Haven't you heard?'

A chill went through Sandra. 'Heard what?' she asked.

'Mrs Roberts died two days ago. She developed pneumonia.'

Afterwards Sandra could scarcely remember how she spent the rest of that day. All the time that she was dealing with other patients she kept seeing Jilly's pale, determined face. Even worse, she could not stop thinking of the two little girls. When she finally finished work at half-past three she put on her coat, said a subdued farewell to the staff who had just come on duty and made her way towards the haematology building. Richard often stopped for a cup of coffee about this time and she felt an urgent need to see him. Just what he could do to make her feel better, she could not imagine, but she wanted to share her grief with him.

Yet when she popped her head around the door of the tea-room only Barry Ripper was present.

'Hi,' he said. 'How's it going?'

'Not too badly,' lied Sandra. 'Barry, have you seen Richard?'

'Sure. He's in his room.'

She almost flew down the corridor. The

door to Richard's office was half open, and her spirits rose. In her soft-soled nursing shoes, she could easily creep in and give him a big surprise. Everything would feel so much better once Richard's arms were around her.

Tiptoeing cautiously forward, she entered the room. But the only person she surprised was herself. Richard was standing with his back to her, leaning over a table. Sandra was on the point of going forward to speak to him when she saw that his arms were around a woman who sat at the table, gazing soulfully up at him. It was Felicity Hamilton.

Hours seemed to have passed by the time Sandra stepped out of her car at Bondi Beach, but it could not have been more than forty minutes. Dusk was approaching and the sea was pewter-grey and turbulent beneath a lowering sky. At the far end of the beach, where the sand gave way to rugged cliffs, huge breakers drove in from the ocean to smash against the rocks in clouds of spray. The mustard-coloured pavilion that was so busy in summer looked forlorn and deserted and a cold wind from the sea blew stinging particles of sand into her eyes. Sea-gulls shrieked overhead, but apart from them the only living creatures were a few hardy joggers. The desolation of the scenery echoed her own mood.

Sandra walked all the way along the beach with her hands dug deep into her pockets, her eyes streaming with the cold and her thoughts in turmoil. She felt completely shattered and disorientated. It wasn't just the shock of Jilly Roberts's death that she had to deal with now. There was also the painful suspicion that Richard was betraying her just at the time when she needed him most. She had seen him putting his arms around Felicity Hamilton with her own eyes, and the whole foundations of her life seemed to be rocked by the revelation. All right, technically she and Richard were not yet lovers, but she was living in his house, they had exchanged intimate kisses and caresses, he had practically told her that he loved her. Didn't that count for anything? Or had she been living in a fool's paradise? She had never wanted to rush their love-making and she had been touched by Richard's willingness to wait. But was he willing to wait simply because he was getting all the satisfaction he needed elsewhere? Sandra groaned aloud.

It was quite dark by the time she returned to the cluster of shops on the esplanade, and her fingers were frozen. The smell of freshly baked cinnamon pastries assaulted her nostrils and hunger swept unexpectedly through her. Turning into a brightly lit plaza, she looked around for a coffee-shop.

'Hello. What are you doing here?' asked a vaguely familiar voice.

She stopped dead and peered uncertainly at the dark-haired man who had spoken to her. Seeing her uncertainty, he grinned and stretched out his hand.

'Ian Finlay from the Nelson Hospital,' he reminded her.

'Oh, of course,' she said, recognising the young doctor, who was a registrar in anaesthetics.

'Your fingers are frozen!' he exclaimed. 'Can I buy you a cup of coffee to warm you up?'

'Thanks. That would be lovely.'

She followed him into a small patisserie and they were soon chatting over coffee and pastries. After the second cup of coffee Ian startled her by asking if she would like to go to the hospital ball with him. A crimson flush swept over Sandra's face. Not wanting to be the subject of gossip at work, she had been careful not to advertise the fact that she was now living with Richard. Suddenly the awkwardness of her position became suddenly clear to her.

'I—I'm sorry, I can't,' she stammered. 'I'm pretty sure I'll be going somebody else.'

'Sure. No worries,' he said easily. 'But if you change your mind let me know, won't you?'

'Yes, of course,' she agreed dully.

She took her leave as soon as possible after that and drove aimlessly around in her car for some time while she tried to collect her scattered thoughts. One thing was obvious: if she had any pride at all, she would have to move out of Richard's place at least until it was clearly established, that there were no other women in his life and that he intended to marry her. And yet the thought of leaving him made a lump rise in her throat.

It was after nine o'clock when she returned home, and Richard was waiting on the front doorstep.

'Where on earth have you been?' he

demanded. 'You never stay out without phoning.'

'Well, I did this time!' snapped Sandra, with the memory of Felicity Hamilton's glossy black hair still fresh in her mind.

He frowned and opened his mouth as if to say more, then seemed to change his mind. 'I've cooked dinner,' he said in an injured tone. 'But it's probably all dried up by now.'

It *was* all dried up, except for the potatoes, which were still half raw. Whatever Richard's talents in the medical field, he was never going to make a good cook. At any other time Sandra would have been touched by his clumsy efforts, but tonight wounded pride made it impossible for her to be gracious. She deliberately pushed her plate away with the charred steak and burnt carrots virtually untouched and the potatoes in a pathetic heap. Richard scowled, but remained silent. It was not until they were sitting in front of the living-room fire, sipping coffee and brandy, that he spoke again. And when he did it was not about food.

'Where were you tonight?' he demanded. 'I was worried about you.'

'Really?' retorted Sandra acidly. 'I would

have thought you'd be far too busy with Felicity Hamilton to spare any time to worry about me.'

'What the hell are you talking about?' he flared.

'You know perfectly well what I'm talking about!' exclaimed Sandra. 'I'm talking about you having your arms around Felicity Hamilton in your office this afternoon.'

'Oh, for heaven's sake!' he snarled. 'Felicity was in my office this afternoon, I'm not denying it, but I certainly didn't have my arms around her.'

'Yes, you did!' she insisted. 'I saw you!'

'And where exactly were you?' demanded Richard with heavy sarcasm. 'On the roof of the casualty building with a pair of binoculars?'

'No!' she snapped. 'I was right there in the room. You left the door open and I came in because I wanted to talk to you about something, but you were too busy canoodling with her even to see me.'

'Oh, yes?' he taunted. 'And where did this canoodling take place? Were we having it off on the bookcases or simply swinging gaily from the chandeliers?'

189

'Oh, shut up!' cried Sandra, biting her knuckles. 'You know perfectly well where you were. Felicity was sitting at the table and you were leaning over her with your arms around her.'

'Oh, I see,' he retorted. 'And did it never occur to you, sweetheart, that Felicity might be sitting at the table because she had a seating plan for the gala dinner open in front of her? Or that I might be leaning over her shoulder pointing out where I wanted the official party to sit?'

Sandra sat still, stricken by a sudden doubt. Before she could speak Richard rose to his feet and paced moodily across to the fireplace. Setting his brandy balloon down on the mantelpiece, he aimed a violent kick at one of the logs, sending up a shower of orange sparks.

'The trouble with you is that you're totally bloody immature!' he shouted, rounding on her. 'You can't even see the truth when it jumps up and hits you in the face. If you were honest with yourself, you'd know damned well that I haven't been playing around with Felicity Hamilton, however many invitations she's been throwing out! What's more, I don't particularly appreciate being treated like some kind of criminal under suspicion.'

There was a moment's frozen silence. Sandra's heart beat frantically as she stared into Richard's face. He looked as though his features were carved out of granite with only his eyes alive. They were like dark pools, dilated wildly in the flickering glare of the flames. Then suddenly his mood changed.

'Look, I'm sorry,' he muttered, running his fingers through his hair. 'I didn't mean to attack you like that, but there really isn't anything between Felicity and me. And I was worried about you when you didn't come home. The roads are wet and I thought you might have had an accident.'

'I'm sorry too,' said Sandra shakily, moving across the floor towards him. 'It's just that I was so upset this afternoon and I wanted to talk to you so badly. Then, finding you like that, I leapt to all the wrong conclusions.'

He put out his hand to her. 'What did you want to talk to me about?' he asked softly.

'Oh, Richard, why—didn't you tell me Jilly Roberts had died?' she faltered.

And with a sudden blind rush she was

in his arms, clinging to him desperately and trying not to cry. He crushed her against him and rocked her from side to side, murmuring low words of comfort and stroking her tumbled hair. She was conscious only of the immense power in his body, the warmth and closeness that he seemed to be offering her with his touch. At that moment she felt certain that Richard was the one man on earth with whom she wanted to share everything, good or bad. Yet, even so, part of her still felt hurt and confused.

'Why didn't you tell me about Jilly?' she repeated.

'You were sick,' he said hoarsely. 'I didn't want to upset you. I meant to tell you this morning before you left for work, but I forgot. I'm sorry.'

Cupping her chin in his hand, he bent and kissed her on the lips. He intended only to comfort her, but somehow they both took fire and the kiss deepened. It was an affirmation of life and warmth and love, a way of shutting out tragedy. Arching her back, Sandra let her whole body curve into his and kissed him with a passion that made him gasp.

He jerked his mouth away from hers

and stared down at her with an anguished expression.

'Don't tempt me, Sandra. I can't bear it!' he muttered savagely.

'I'm not just tempting you!' she replied shakily. 'You always said you'd wait until I was ready, Richard. And I'm ready now.'

His arms came round her like steel cables and he hugged her against him, crushing the breath out of her.

'Do you mean that?' he demanded hoarsely.

'Yes!' she insisted.

'Oh, God, Sandra, you're the finest woman in the world!'

His lips found hers, urgent, warm, demanding, and she kissed him back with a hunger that shocked and enthralled him. Threading his fingers through her blonde curls, he tilted her head back so that he could drop feather-light kisses on her throat. Sandra uttered a low moan of longing and suddenly they both blazed up with desire. Richard's powerful hands moved urgently over her body and he drew her down to the floor. Seizing her uniform by the bodice, he unbuttoned it slowly and sensually and then peeled it away from her body. In the amber glow of the firelight her slim shoulders and gently swelling breasts gleamed like satin.

'Oh, Sandra, you're so beautiful,' he breathed.

With a swift, decisive movement, he reached for the lace hem of her teddy and pulled it over her head. It never occurred to her to resist. What was happening to her now seemed more right and natural than anything she had ever experienced. A strong, pulsing heat was beginning to grow deep inside her and she was conscious only of wanting Richard. Wanting him with an urgency that made her ache and quiver under his touch. And when he unhitched the flimsy bra and flung it away she arched her back, deliberately offering him her warm, tender breasts.

'Oh, Richard,' she gasped. 'Oh, my love.'

His lips moved urgently over her skin and thrill after thrill of excitement rippled through her body. Then he raised his head and looked down at her, his face tense and strange with urgency.

'Do you want me to stop?' he said hoarsely. 'Because if you do tell me now. Any more of this and it will be too late...'

Sandra smiled at him mistily, conscious that it was already too late. A surge of pride and love crested through her as she saw his powerful, masculine body outlined with the orange glow of the fire. He's mine, she thought triumphantly. And, after tonight nobody will ever be able to take him away from me. Reaching up her hands, she slipped them inside his shirt and caressed his muscular shoulders.

'Don't stop, Richard,' she whispered. 'I want you just as much as you want me. More.'

'Are you sure?' he growled, tidying a stray curl back from her cheek.

'I'm sure.'

With a quick, ragged breath, he set to work to undress her. Then, kneeling in front of her, he gazed exultantly at her naked, youthful body.

Colour washed into her face, but she returned his gaze steadily enough. 'Your turn,' she reminded him huskily.

Rising to his feet with lithe, animal grace, he hauled his shirt forward over his head and dropped it on the floor. His shoes and socks were scuffed carelessly aside, then his hands went to his belt-buckle. As he stood there, towering over her, Sandra thought, with a shock of astonishment, how magnificent he looked. His body was lean and hard and rippling with muscle and the hairs on his chest gleamed like bronze. He stood for a moment, staring down at her with narrowed, tawny eyes. Then slowly, almost challengingly, he unzipped his trousers and stepped out of them. She made a soft, choked sound in the back of her throat.

In a single fluid movement, he was on his knees beside her. His arms came round her, crushing her against him, and he buried his face in her hair. With merciless sensuality he began nuzzling her neck, dropping brief, unsatisfying kisses on her throat and ear-lobes and shoulders. Then, with a purposeful gleam in his eyes, he thrust her back so that she lay sprawled on the carpet, and began to kiss his way teasingly down her body. And what kisses they were! Now and then he stopped to rub his thick gold hair teasingly across her naked body, making her gasp and writhe with ticklish delight. But most of the time he was content to leave trails of fire on her skin with his warm lips and tongue.

At last she could bear it no longer and drew him back up to meet her, welcoming him with parted lips and eager, caressing hands. Their lips met and they kissed deeply, sensually, until Richard suddenly caught her off guard and imprisoned her in his arms. Rolling chaotically, they fetched up so close to the fire that Sandra could feel the fierce heat of the flames dancing on her skin. Richard raised himself on one elbow and gazed down with glittering golden eyes into her flushed face.

'I can't wait another moment,' he said hoarsely.

She could not hold back a gasp of dismay as he entered her, but after the first pain and shock her body began to move slowly, tentatively in rhythm with his. His lips touched her hair, his words of endearment were breathed disjointedly into her ear and slowly her panic receded and her body opened gladly, warmly, to welcome him in. Arching her back, she offered herself to him and found that there was a surprising, sensual delight in these violent encounters. For a long time they shifted and murmured, exploring each other's bodies and glorying in each new touch and caress. Then Sandra heard Richard's breathing quicken and, to her astonishment, she felt an unknown urgency begin to build inside her like the relentless roar of surf, pounding on a deserted beach. For a moment she rode with it, swept up in a dizzy excitement, then the feeling receded, paused and came thudding back in stupefying grandeur.

'Richard! Oh, Richard!' she cried.

And, turning her face into his shoulder, she clung to him and closed her eyes. A moment later she felt rather than heard his strangled cry of fulfilment, then he was crushing her against him, burying his face in her hair, holding her as if he would never let her go.

'I love you, Sandra,' he said with a deep, shuddering breath. 'I'll never want another woman as long as I live!'

CHAPTER TEN

If Sandra hoped for a dramatic change in her relationship with Richard in the weeks that followed she was doomed to disappointment. Of course there was a new level of intimacy between them. Richard proved to be a magnificent lover, passionate, inventive and wildly exciting. And yet any display of emotion seemed to horrify him. It was true that he had told her he loved her, but Sandra suspected that the statement was meaningless. Certainly he never repeated it, and she couldn't help wondering if he regretted ever saying it. Yet she was determined not to press him on the subject. Richard had always made it clear that deep involvements weren't his style. Well, she would be modern and cool and sophisticated, just the way he wanted.

It was a decision that did not go down at all well with her brother Mario. Mario still viewed Richard with bitter suspicion and, although he could not actually challenge him to a duel, he did the next best thing. He banned him from his house.

'When that swine puts a ring on your finger he'll be welcome in my house, but not before!' he told Sandra with his jaw thrust out.

This meant that Sandra now saw little of her brother, since she refused to visit him without Richard, but the clash of loyalties upset her. Fortunately Lisa and Tony didn't share Mario's archaic views and they made frequent—and probably forbidden—visits to Richard's house. Both of them liked Richard and, when his birthday arrived, they brought presents for him. Knowing that birthday celebrations had been few and far between in his life, Sandra decided to make the day a special occasion for him. When he came downstairs to breakfast he found the dining-table set with the best china and an impressive array of his favourite foods in silver chafing-dishes and crystal bowls.

'What's all this?' he demanded, pausing on the threshold of the room. 'Have I wandered into the wrong house? Where's the Nescafé and mouldy toast we usually have for breakfast?'

'You beast!' exclaimed Sandra. 'I've never given you mouldy toast.'

'Well, maybe not. But why the state banquet? Is the Queen coming for break-fast?'

'No!' she cried impatiently. 'It's your birthday, of course.'

'My birthday?' he echoed with a startled expression. 'How did you know it was my birthday?'

'You told me once when I was reading

the horoscopes out of the newspaper. Now sit down and eat before it all gets cold. And happy birthday.'

She kissed him on the cheek. Richard looked embarrassed, but pleased. As he took his place at the end of the table he gazed questioningly at the pile of presents beside his plate. 'Are these for me too?' he asked.

'Yes. But eat your breakfast first. I'm afraid the eggs Benedict will spoil if they're left much longer.'

'This looks superb,' he sighed rapturously, taking the lid off one of the silver dishes. 'Now what are all these things?'

'Most of it's pretty obvious,' replied Sandra. 'Fresh honeydew and cantaloupe melon, muesli, grilled bacon, sausages, scrambled eggs, eggs Benedict—they're the poached eggs on muffins with the asparagus and hollandaise sauce. Toast, croissants, orange juice and coffee.'

For fifteen minutes they ate in blissful silence. Then at last Richard wiped his mouth, set down his empty orange-juice glass and gave a contented sigh.

'You're a five-star girlfriend, Sandra,' he said reverently. 'I don't deserve you.'

'No, you don't,' she agreed tranquilly,

stacking the empty dishes. 'But I suppose you're just lucky.'

'I certainly am,' he muttered, gazing after her as she carried the tray out to the kitchen. 'Luckier than I ever realised.'

'What did you say?' asked Sandra, reappearing through the swinging door with a percolator full of hot coffee.

'Nothing,' he replied. 'But I'll tell you this, Sandra. Your blood's worth bottling.'

She looked at him with comic horror.

'Oh, no, you don't!' she cried. 'You're not getting a standard four hundred and thirty donation from me today. This is definitely my day off.'

'Yes. Rather clever of me to have my birthday on a Saturday when we were both off duty, wasn't it?' demanded Richard smugly. 'Now, when do I get to open my presents?'

'Right away,' replied Sandra. The bottle-shaped one is from me, the large box is from Lisa and the small lopsided one is from Tony.'

Richard stared at her in disbelief. 'You mean Lisa and Tony bought me presents too?' he asked.

'Yes. Well, as Lisa said, you're practically family. Oh, don't stare at me like that,

Richard. Open them.'

Still eyeing Sandra thoughtfully, Richard slowly peeled the brightly coloured wrapping paper off her present, revealing a handsome leather-covered wine jug with a brass lion's head on one side and a long chain curving from the cork at the top into the lion's mouth.

'Do you like it?' she asked anxiously. 'I bought it last summer in Florence.'

'It's beautiful,' he replied simply. 'Thank you, Sandra.'

He came around the table and kissed her before opening the second parcel. This contained a set of matching leather-covered glasses with a card in Lisa's flowing handwriting.

'How nice of her,' said Richard. 'Now what's this?' He picked up the lumpy parcel which was Tony's offering and shook it for clues.

'Don't expect too much,' warned Sandra. 'He's learning pottery at school and he made it himself. It's a coffee-mug, I believe.'

He opened the card and read it aloud.

To Uncle Richard with love from Tony. xxx

His eyebrows shot up at the words, 'Uncle Richard', but he said nothing until the present was unwrapped. 'Good God!' he breathed as the last layer of red tissue paper peeled away, revealing an extraordinary creation covered in a bright blue glaze. On the side was a large white letter 'R'.

The young potter evidently hadn't fully mastered the skills of his craft, for the handle was distinctly cockeyed, the rim was lumpy and covered with fingerprints and the whole mug wobbled precariously on its base when touched. What was worse, the opening at the top was only the size of a fairly small coin. Richard let out a smothered hoot of laughter.

'Do you suppose it's possible to drink out of this?' he demanded.

Sandra's lips quivered.

'You'd probably be taking your life in your hands,' she said. 'But you could always try.'

She passed the coffee percolator across to him.

'Put plenty of milk in,' she advised. 'Then you won't get scalded if it leaks.'

It didn't leak. It cascaded. The moment

Richard lifted it to his lips a stream of tan liquid poured down the front of his shirt. Leaping to his feet with a startled oath, he snatched a napkin and mopped himself dry.

'There was a crooked man, who walked a crooked mile, and drank some crooked coffee, while he smiled a crooked smile!' he improvised bitterly, hauling his shirt over his head. 'No, it's definitely not a working model, Sandra.'

She looked at him anxiously.

'You won't throw it away, will you?' she asked.

'What, and have his aunt come after me tooth and claw?' retorted Richard. 'No, sweetheart, I won't throw it away. I'm beginning to realise that when you get involved with a Calvi you're taking on a package deal with the whole clan. And I certainly don't want to hurt your feelings or Tony's.'

He vanished into the kitchen, rinsed out the mug, dried it and returned. Then, after a moment's thoughtful silence, he set it on the mantelpiece and dropped a couple of packets of matches inside.

'There you are,' he said. 'Useful and beautiful. Besides, I'm quite touched by it, really. It's the first time in twenty years that anyone's given me a birthday present.' He grinned widely. 'And what a present!' he added.

Not long after this Sandra was transferred for a two-month stint in Casualty. It was a move that suited her. Although the accident and emergency work could be harrowing there, was little chance to form attachments to patients. She knew she had made a mistake in allowing herself to become so fond of Jilly Roberts and she felt that a change of scene could only do her good. Yet she had only been in Casualty for a few days when a patient was brought in with whom she had a very strong bond indeed: Tony.

'Oh, no!' she exclaimed when she saw the curly-haired child arrive in the custody of two ambulance officers. 'What on earth have you been up to?'

Tony flashed her a guilty smile.

'I was playing basketball and I fell and banged my elbow,' he explained.

'Basketball!' she echoed in horror. 'You shouldn't have been doing that!'

'I know,' he admitted as she took him into the assessment-room. 'But we had a relief teacher and he didn't know I was a haemophiliac, so he let me. It was fun until I fell.'

'What's going on here?' asked Sister Wright, the duty sister, appearing at the bedside. 'Who is this child?'

'He's my nephew, Tony Calvi,' explained Sandra hastily. 'He's bumped his elbow and he's a severe haemophiliac with a baseline Factor VIII level of less than one per cent. If there's bleeding into the joint, he'll need that raised to about twenty-five per cent for two or three days. He'll almost certainly have to have cryo, administered through a drip. But I think we'd better call Dr Daly.'

'Have we got his records on computer here?' asked Sister Wright.

'Yes,' replied Sandra.

'Good. Well, that should speed things up considerably.'

It did. Richard soon arrived and after a X-ray had shown that there was no fracture he confirmed that there was a haemarthrosis.

'Now, let's see, what's his body weight?' he asked.

'About thirty kilos,' replied Sandra promptly.

He frowned as he did a rapid calculation.

'In that case he'll need, say, three hundred and seventy-five units of Factor VIII. There are a hundred units to a bag of cryoprecipitate, so four bags of cryo should do it, delivered through a drip. He should have the initial loading dose after the first six hours and then every twelve hours as long as is needed to control the haemorrhage. Have his parents been notified that he's here?'

'Tony said the school tried to ring Lisa, but she must have been out shopping, and Mario's in rehearsal and can't get away. I'll try again soon.'

It was after five o'clock when Lisa arrived, looking flustered. Once she had been reassured by a visit to the children's ward Sandra invited her home for a drink.

'I do wish Mario would give up on this idea of going to Italy.' Lisa said unhappily when they were all in Richard's living-room, sipping sherry. 'It's pure madness, with Tony's condition as it is. But Mario's so stubborn about it. I wouldn't mind so much if he'd just agree to take us for two weeks in the school holidays at the beginning of July. You'll be there then, won't you, Sandra?'

Sandra hesitated, then nodded.

'Yes,' she said with a sigh. 'But I won't be staying long. Just a couple of weeks to see Mamma. I'm not staying on for the summer opera season.'

'That's the whole trouble!' said Lisa bitterly. 'Mario wants us to stay on until he finishes performing at the end of September. You won't be there, and I don't blame you! But what am I to do if Tony hurts himself in that time?'

'Well, you'll just have to be firm and refuse to stay,' replied Sandra.

Lisa rolled her eyes. 'That's more easily said than done with Mario!' she retorted.

After Lisa had left Sandra sat with a pensive look on her face. She couldn't help worrying about the problems of her brother's family, which seemed no closer than ever to being resolved. Richard came across to join her and ruffled her hair.

'You are off duty this Sunday, aren't you? Because, if you are, I thought I might take you to lunch at Tarquinio's and really lash out a bit.'

Her frown vanished.

'That would be lovely, Richard,' she agreed. 'Thank you. Sister Wright did ask me if I could do some overtime in

Casualty, since they're so short-staffed, but I'll tell her I'm not available.'

'Good. And, seeing it's such a nice evening for a change, why don't we go out on the terrace?'

They were just in time to watch the sunset over the harbour. Sandra sat in a salmon-pink lounging-chair, with a pair of binoculars trained on the water traffic, while Richard flicked idly through one of her gardening catalogues. From inside the house a strong aroma of chicken stew drifted enticingly forth, while down below they could hear the hiss and wash of the waves slapping against the rocky shore. A sea-gull glided lazily overhead, its feathers gilded by the setting sun, and two houses away they could hear the laughter of playing children. Sandra lowered her binoculars and let a quiet sense of contentment wash over her. For the first time in her life she was experiencing the profound but simple joy of a man and woman living together. If only Richard would make a real commitment to her, life would be utterly perfect.

He saw her wistful smile and reached out and touched her cheek.

'Happy?' he asked, staring intently into her blue eyes.

'Yes,' she said, with only a hint of a sigh. 'Are you?'

By way of reply he rose from his chair, then crouched down beside her. Running his fingers through her hair, he suddenly cupped her face in his hands and kissed her fiercely on the mouth.

'I don't think I've ever been happier in my life,' he said in a harsh voice, as if the admission was torn out of him unwillingly. 'The house used to be so shuttered and silent, but now I can't get home quickly enough, knowing that you're here.'

She opened her mouth to speak, but before she could say a word he was on his feet again and moving rapidly away from her.

'Would you like another drink?' he asked casually, with one of those lightning-swift changes of mood that she found so disconcerting.

She wanted to leap to her feet and run after him, fling her arms around him and cry, 'Richard, I love you. And I'm sure you love me, so why do you keep fighting it?' Yet she sensed that would only antagonise him. If Richard was ever going to admit his need for her, the first move would have to come from him.

'Yes, please,' she replied, striving to keep her tone as light as his. 'Campari and soda, if we've got any. And then I must rescue that stew before it sticks to the bottom of the pan.'

The Campari was delicious, bitter-sweet and slightly astringent. By the time they had finished their drinks dusk had fallen and the evening air was growing cooler, but they were both reluctant to go inside.

'How about eating under the loggia?' asked Richard. 'The stucco walls trap the heat from the sun, so it should be quite warm there. And we can watch the stars come out.'

'Good idea,' agreed Sandra. 'If you'll set the table up, I'll bring the food out.'

They began with a simple Italian antipasto of mortadella sausage, provolone cheese, green olives and a few pickled vegetables. Then Sandra brought a huge casserole full of chicken stew with mushrooms, white wine and potatoes in it, accompanied by a side-dish of green beans. Richard opened a bottle of Riesling and they ate slowly, savouring the aromatic food and the light, dry wine. Sandra picked up the bottle and scrutinised the label.

'Mmm, it's good,' she said critically. 'But not as good as the white wine we drink in Orvieto. Now that is pure poetry! I can't wait to taste it again when I go back in July to visit Mamma.'

Richard twirled his glass and took a thoughtful sip.

'So you really are going as usual this year?' he asked.

'Oh, yes,' she answered with a smile. 'I couldn't possibly miss it—Mamma would be so disappointed. But I'll only be staying for two weeks this year. I couldn't get any more leave than that from the hospital, since I've only been working such a short time.'

Richard set his knife and fork together with a sigh of pleasure and dabbed his lips with a napkin.

'That stew was superb,' he told her simply.

She twinkled at him.

'I'm glad you think so,' she retorted. 'I've made so much that we'll probably be eating it for the next two weeks.'

And then Richard said something which drove all thoughts of stew out of her mind.

'How would you feel about it if I came to Italy with you?' he asked abruptly.

Sandra felt as if a trapdoor had suddenly opened beneath her, letting her drop ten feet to land with a jolt.

'I'd be delighted,' she replied warily. 'And I'm sure my mother would be happy to have you to stay.' A faint flush mounted to her face and she went on hastily, 'I'm afraid we couldn't share a room, though. She's old and rather conservative. I couldn't embarrass her like that.'

Richard's hand covered hers and he squeezed her fingers warmly.

'No, of course,' he agreed. 'I wouldn't want you to. But are you sure I wouldn't be intruding on a family gathering?'

'No, we'd love to have you,' protested Sandra swiftly. And then honesty overtook her. 'Well, I'd love to have you and I'm sure Mamma would. Mario might be a bit of a problem, but I think he'd keep his temper under control, since it's not his own household. Although, of course, I couldn't promise it.'

He chuckled throatily. 'I think it would improve Mario's character to be polite to me for two weeks,' he said provocatively.

'Ah,' she retorted. 'And what would

214

it do for your character to be polite to him?'

Richard sipped his wine and gave her a slow, teasing smile.

'But my character doesn't need any improvement, does it?' he demanded.

'You conceited beast!' cried Sandra. 'I suppose you'll tell me next that you have every virtue known to man? Modesty included?'

His face was suddenly serious.

'No,' he said. 'But I will tell you this, Sandra. If you really think having me there will cause too much ill feeling, I could wait and go with you some time when Mario won't be there. Say, next year.'

She suffered another heart-stopping jolt at these words. *Next year.* It was the first time Richard had ever hinted that their relationship might last beyond their next passionate encounter. Somehow the suggestion set up a painful, fluttering hope in her heart.

'Do you think we'll still be together next year?' she asked in a troubled voice.

His fingers crushed hers. 'God, I hope so,' he said vehemently. 'I can't imagine how I'd get along without you now, Sandra.'

She gazed at him with misty eyes and leaned slowly forward. But at that promising moment the telephone rang.

'Damn!' growled Richard, flinging down his napkin. 'Don't bother, I'll get it.'

He was gone for nearly ten minutes and, when he came back, he wore a wry expression.

'Can we take a rain-check on that lunch we were planning?' he asked. 'Some hospital business has come up which I'll just have to deal with, and Sunday is the only free time I've got.'

The earlier mood of intimacy was gone, and Sandra did not attempt to recapture it.

'Oh, no!' she exclaimed in disgust. 'All right, Richard, But only on condition that you take me out on your next free day.'

'Scout's honour,' he agreed with a quirky grin, holding up three fingers. 'Dib, dob, dub, or whatever they say.'

Sandra rose from her chair with a sigh and began stacking plates.

'Well, if you're going to be working, I certainly won't want to mope around here on my own,' she said. 'I'll go and ring Cathy Wright and tell her I can do overtime on Sunday after all.'

Sunday afternoon in Casualty proved to be too busy to allow Sandra a single moment to mope over Richard. A cardiac arrest involved a tense period in the triage unit, using a defibrillator on a forty-two-year-old father of three who had keeled over on a golf course. And then there was a nine-year-old Vietnamese boy, who had fallen off his bike coming down a hill and was carried in from the ambulance covered in blood and grit and sobbing with pain. An X-ray revealed a supracondylar fracture of the humerus, which carried a risk of irritation to the brachial artery, thus causing Volkman's ischaemic contracture.

Once the doctor on duty had set the arm Sandra had to phone the children's ward and arrange admission for forty-eight hours for careful monitoring. After that she faced the far more daunting task of trying to outline the problem to an anxious mother who knew little English. In the end she had to use the telephone interpreter service to explain the importance of keeping the child for observation of the radial pulse, pain in the forearm, the colour, warmth and sensation in the fingers and other signs which could indicate trouble.

After that she had to deal in quick succession with a child who had swallowed an upholstery pin, a toddler with a middle-ear infection and a group of teenagers who had rolled their car but miraculously escaped with only cuts and abrasions. And just when she was settling down for a well-earned cup of coffee a man arrived who had been mowing his lawn in thongs and had run over his toe. By the time Sandra arrived home she was limp with exhaustion and beginning to wish she had taken up lion-taming or some other easy job as a career.

To her disappointment Richard was not at home. She felt too tired to face a large meal, so she made do with a roll and some salad on a tray in front of the television and went to bed early. When Richard tiptoed in, some time after midnight, she simply sighed and turned over, and when she rose at six, to get ready for work, he was still asleep.

'Oh, when do doctors and nurses ever get to see their families?' she muttered resentfully, as she tightened the belt around her slim waist and set her cap straight. 'I'll catch up with you at lunchtime, darling. All right?'

As she bent to kiss him he murmured something inaudible about the hospital canteen, then vanished again in an avalanche of blankets. Smiling indulgently, Sandra patted his shoulder—or perhaps it was his chest, she wasn't really sure—looked at the clock and bolted for the door.

Her morning in Casualty passed tranquilly, and she was humming as she made her way to the staff canteen at twelve o'clock. Although the silver birch trees in the hospital grounds were now almost bare the autumn sun was mild and golden. Sandra felt glad to be alive, and she was totally unaware of the shock that was awaiting her in the canteen. Threading her way through the busy throng of people inside, she grabbed a tray and stood in line near the hot buffet. As the queue moved slowly forward, she scanned the long room, hoping for a glimpse of Richard. But there was no sign of him.

'What'll it be, love?'

The voice from the plump woman behind the counter brought her back to earth.

'Oh, the lasagne, please.'

It definitely wasn't lasagne like Mamma used to make, but Sandra was too hungry to be fussy. Making her way past the check-out, she looked around for an empty seat.

'Hey, Sandra, come and join me!'

The red-haired nurse Laura Maddox was grinning invitingly over the top of a newspaper. Rather reluctantly Sandra picked her way across to join her. Laura was friendly enough, but definitely a gossip, and the last thing Sandra wanted was to be interrogated about her love-life.

'Hello, Laura. How are you?' she said guardedly.

'Oh, fine. And how are you? Got any sexy new boyfriends?'

'No—' began Sandra.

And then stopped. For at that moment Richard walked into the canteen, accompanied by Felicity Hamilton and a glamorous middle-aged woman who looked like an older version of her. An inexplicable chill ran down Sandra's spine. There was no reason why Richard shouldn't be in the hospital canteen with another doctor, yet she couldn't banish the ominous sense of dismay that swept through her.

'Are you all right?' asked Laura. 'You look quite pale.'

'Do I?' said Sandra with a forced laugh. 'Starvation, I expect. I'll just put my tray back and do something about it.'

Pushing her way through the crowd in a ruthless manner that was quite unlike her, she managed to reach Richard just as he was ushering Felicity and the other woman into the buffet queue ahead of him. Touching his arm, she spoke in a low, urgent tone.

'Richard, I need to talk to you.'

'Not now, Sandra,' he hissed. 'I'm busy with the Hamiltons.'

'After lunch, then?'

'No! I'll be tied up with them for another couple of hours. Now be a good girl and shove off, will you?'

Taking her tray out of her nerveless fingers, he thrust it on the pile and gave her a surreptitious push. Sandra was so shocked that she was halfway down the canteen before she even looked back. By then Richard was leaning down attentively over Felicity's dark head as she pointed at something on the buffet. And his hand, she noticed bitterly, was holding Felicity's elbow with tender solicitude. Tears of rage and dismay scalded her eyelids, but she blinked them away as she marched back to her table.

'Isn't that Richard Daly down there?' asked Laura, craning her neck.

'Mm,' agreed Sandra, suppressing a powerful urge to open her mouth and howl.

'Didn't you go out with him once?'

'Yes.'

With that curt reply Sandra opened her mouth and thrust in such a large forkful of lasagne that she would have a good excuse not to talk for the next five minutes. Unfortunately it was so hot that it blistered her palate, and she gave a choking gulp. Laura looked at her curiously.

'Here, have some water,' she offered, passing a carafe.

There was silence for a moment while Sandra tried to swallow the hot food and Laura watched her closely.

'Didn't it work out with you and Richard?' she asked with interest, the moment Sandra could speak.

'No,' said Sandra in a choked voice, 'it didn't work out.'

'Probably just as well, really,' said Laura sagely. 'If you ask me, he and Felicity

Hamilton deserve each other. Well, they're both the same sort, aren't they? Chew people up and then spit them out when they're finished. Mind you, they do seem to be serious about each other, which is pretty amazing. I mean, look at the way they were carrying on at that lunch yesterday—twined around each other like a pair of octopuses!'

A chill feeling settled in Sandra's stomach.

'What lunch?' she asked.

By way of reply, Laura folded her newpaper and passed it across the table.

'That lunch!' she said triumphantly, stabbing her finger at a large photo splashed across the social page.

With a sensation of mounting dread Sandra looked down at the photo. It showed Richard Daly and Felicity Hamilton, both flashing radiant smiles amid the ambience of an elegant restaurant. Their arms were around each other and there was an air of possessive warmth in the way Felicity's long, slender fingers rested caressingly on Richard's shoulder. Leaning on the backs of their chairs and gazing fondly down at them was the middle-aged woman who now sat at Richard's table, further down the cafeteria. For a moment the print bluffed before Sandra's eyes, then she forced herself to read the caption.

Caught enjoying an intimate lunch at the new Tarquinio's restaurant, overlooking the harbour, are Mrs Diana Hamilton of Vaucluse, her daughter Dr Felicity Hamilton and close friend Dr Richard Daly.

Close friend! thought Sandra furiously. Very close. Close enough to push me out of my lunch date and take her instead. I could kill him for this, the swine! And her. Hospital business! Ha!

'Old Ma Hamilton must be pleased with the way things are coming on,' remarked Laura. 'She's been angling to get Richard Daly as a son-in-law for months, from all I hear.'

Sandra stuck her fork savagely into the steaming mound of lasagne and rose to her feet.

'I've burnt my mouth too badly to eat the rest of this,' she said abruptly. 'I think I'll just get back to work. See you later, Laura.'

As she walked past Richard's table she

caught his eye and gave him a look of burning reproach. He looked baffled for a moment, then shrugged carelessly and turned his attention back to Felicity. If Sandra had owned a sub-machine gun, she would have strafed the pair of them with it, but as it was she simply had to walk the agonising distance to the door.

All afternoon she brooded over what she had learnt. Even setting aside Laura's comments, the picture looked black enough. Richard had broken his date with her simply in order to take Felicity and her mother to lunch. Worse than that, he had lied to her about it, saying that he was tied up with hospital business. Could she ever trust him again?

CHAPTER ELEVEN

On the way home Sandra stopped at a news stand and bought a copy of the offending paper. Absurdly, she turned to the social pages with shaking fingers, as if she thought some miracle might have happened. Perhaps the photo that had upset her so much would have been replaced by a harmless portrait of the Hamiltons with some unknown mining magnate. But Richard still smiled treacherously up at her from the page and his arm still rested lovingly around Felicity's shoulders. Flinging the newspaper into the car, Sandra climbed listlessly in after it. What on earth should she do? Throwing away her pride to live with a man was one thing. But throwing away her pride to let him take another mistress? All her hot Italian blood rose to the surface.

'Never!' she vowed, as she turned the ignition on with a savage movement. 'I'll kill him first!'

By the time Richard arrived home that evening she had decided what she was going to do. Even so, she could not repress a foolish, fluttering hope as she heard his key in the front door. He didn't behave like a man haunted by guilt. She heard the heavy thud as he dropped a briefcase on the floor and a lighter thud as he flung an armful of papers on the hall table.

'Honey, I'm home!' he called.

There was a pause.

'Sandra?'

She heard him going from room to

room, and at last, when he approached the casual family room opening on to the loggia, her strained nerves could stand it no longer.

'I'm here!' she said sharply.

The door opened and he stood there, looking so much his normal self that a pang went through her. His tawny eyes kindled as he saw her and the lopsided smile lit his face. It was all she could do to stop herself running into his arms.

'Don't I get a kiss?' he asked, frowning.

Her heart hammered furiously and her mouth felt suddenly dry. She had to remind herself savagely of his treachery with Felicity.

'I'm leaving!' she blurted out.

His look of consternation was so intense that it could not possibly have been faked. For an instant he stood staring at her with a dazed expression, then his mouth tightened grimly.

'Why?' he rapped out.

Sandra's hand shook as she held out the newspaper to him.

'This is why!' she replied hoarsely.

He took a swift glance at the photo, gave a derisive snort, ripped the newspaper in half, then in quarters, and flung it

227

contemptuously on the floor.

'I asked you why,' he said through his teeth.

'And I told you!' retorted Sandra with a tremor in her voice.

'No, you didn't!' he whipped back. 'You showed me a photo of myself with two women. That explains nothing to me.'

'Oh, come off it!' she cried with heavy sarcasm. 'You invited me to lunch on Sunday, Richard! And then suddenly you had a phone call telling you that you had urgent hospital business that required your attention on Sunday. What exactly was the urgent hospital business that required your attention at Tarquinio's, Richard? Were you performing a lumbar puncture on Dr Hamilton? Or testing her for aplastic anaemia? Or were there actually a whole lot of packed red cells in that innocent-looking champagne bottle? Were you in fact performing a life-saving blood transfusion on your "close friend" Felicity?'

'No, I wasn't!' flared Richard. 'For heaven's sake, Sandra, stop being so stupid and jealous and immature! You sound like some wronged wife in a soapie.'

'Oh, do I?' demanded Sandra angrily. 'Well, I'd have a great chance of being any kind of a wife around you, Richard, wronged or otherwise. Because you're not really into marriage, are you? Stuff like fidelity and commitment and loyalty is really only for raw-boned peasants from Orvieto, isn't it? The kind of people who are stupid and jealous and immature enough to think that if you're living with one woman it's pretty tasteless to be involved with another on the sly.'

'God Almighty!' roared Richard. 'How many times do I have to tell you that I am *not* involved with Felicity Hamilton?'

'You can tell me as many times as you want,' retorted Sandra sweetly, tapping her foot. 'Of course, whether I believe you or not is another matter.'

'Oh, never mind about Felicity!' exclaimed Richard impatiently, seizing her by the shoulders. 'That's not what's really griping you, is it? It's the fact that I haven't asked you to marry me, isn't it?'

'No!' said Sandra with her nose in the air. 'Why should that bother me? What makes you think that I want to marry you, anyway? I wouldn't marry you if you were the last man alive!'

Richard ignored this meaningless babble

and pulled her closer with a grip so tight that it hurt her.

'Look,' he urged, staring down at her with blazing gold eyes. 'Try to understand, Sandra. You come from a stable home; it's easy and natural for you to think in terms of marriage. It isn't for me. I never had a father around the place, and my one and only attempt at marriage was a total disaster. The whole idea just scares the hell out of me. But you are special to me. I would never have asked you to live with me otherwise. After all, it did seem like the easiest way of checking out our feelings for each other.'

'Sure,' agreed Sandra bitterly. 'Easy and natural, with a foolproof money-back guarantee if it doesn't work. Except that people aren't made like that, Richard. Or I'm not anyway. I'm just not into love without commitment.'

'And you think I am?' he demanded harshly.

'It's difficult to think anything else, isn't it?' she parried. 'Especially when you're swanning around with good old Felicity on the sly. I was a fool ever to trust you, Richard. Mario warned me what it would be like.'

Richard's mouth hardened. Dropping her arm, he paced across the room, then swung round with an angry glint in his tawny eyes.

'I thought it wouldn't be long before we got back to big brother Mario laying down the law,' he retorted bitterly. 'And just what did dear Mario have to say on that subject, may I ask?'

'Yes, you may!' cried Sandra hotly. 'But you can stop talking about him in that poisonous tone of voice. I know you don't like Mario, but he's my brother and he's always done his best for me. I don't suppose it means anything to you, Richard, but I've flown in the face of all my family's values to come and live with you. And where did it get me? Nowhere! It's all turned out just the way Mario said it would. He told me you'd be sleeping with other women before I knew where I was!'

'Well, if you believe that, there's nothing more to be said, is there?' he demanded in a hard voice.

Sandra drew in a deep, shaky breath and tossed her head.

'No, I suppose there's not,' she agreed in a wavering voice. 'I might just as well leave. Unless you've got some brilliant explanation that you're going to pull out of a hat?'

She looked at him with almost a pleading expression and for a moment he seemed on the brink of saying something. Then his mouth closed tightly and a muscle twitched in his cheek.

'Well?' she challenged.

'No,' he said coldly. 'I don't think I'll pull any rabbits out of hats for you, Sandra. After all, you've obviously made up your mind that I can't be trusted, so the magic wouldn't last long, would it? Why don't you just go ahead and leave? Do us both a favour!'

When Sandra slammed the door of her car and staggered inside her brother's house with an armful of belongings she found the family sitting at dinner. She would have crept straight upstairs without speaking, but as she passed the dining-room door a book slid from under her chin and crashed to the floor. Everyone looked up.

'Sandra!' cried Lisa. 'How nice to see you! Is Richard with you?'

'No!' snapped Sandra. 'I've left him!'

A startled look passed between the

adults. Then Mario rose to his feet, crossed the room and kissed her warmly on both cheeks.

'*Brava!*' he exclaimed. 'You did the right thing, *cara*. He was not worthy of you—I always told you so.'

'Oh, shut up Mario!' flared Sandra. 'There's no need to be so damned self-satisfied.'

'Well, I think you're mean!' piped up Tony. 'I liked Richard, and he said he'd take me out in his boat next weekend. And now I bet he won't. I hate you, Sandra!'

'Tony!' reproached Lisa. 'Don't speak to your aunt like that. Now sit up straight and eat your spaghetti. Sandra, do you want some dinner?'

Sandra's lip quivered.

'I'm not hungry!' she said in a muffled voice, and fled upstairs.

The next three weeks were a difficult time for Sandra. Her anger and resentment towards Richard still smouldered fiercely and she felt certain she had done the right thing by leaving him. Whatever she might have told him, she had to admit that Richard had put his finger on the problem. She did want him to marry her,

233

but that was obviously a commitment that he wasn't prepared to make. End of story. Except that Sandra found it impossible to put him out of her mind. At night she had trouble sleeping, but when she did doze off her sleep was filled with turbulent dreams in which Richard shouted angrily at her—or, worse still, made love to her with a tenderness and passion that brought her awake with tears on her cheeks.

She could not even glimpse a golden-haired man in a crowd without an uprush of excitement followed by an immediate pang of disappointment. Working at the hospital was the worst part of all, for the glimpses were so apt to be the real thing. By common consent they kept their professional meetings brisk and frigidly polite, but Sandra found the chance encounters in corridors or the canteen overwhelmingly painful. In the end she completely stopped going to the hospital canteen. Anyway, she never really felt hungry any more.

Yet, if work made her miserable, it also provided the only solace that kept her going through this difficult period. At least she could forget all about her own problems while she was immersed in hospital routine. Compared to the life and death struggles of some of the patients, what did her trivial difficulties matter anyway? And, since she no longer felt the slightest interest in social life, it made sense to take on as much overtime work as she could. Or so she thought.

Her family did not agree. Mario and Lisa were becoming increasingly worried about the shadows under her eyes, her lack of appetite and her general air of listlessness. If Lisa could have waved a magic wand, she would have transported Sandra and Richard instantly to a desert island to work out their differences. Mario's solution was different. He was convinced that, if only Sandra would give up her job at the hospital and come on tour with Tony again, everybody would live happily ever after. And he spent every spare moment trying to overcome Sandra's opposition to the idea. Consequently, when Sandra was woken by a knock at her bedroom door one Saturday morning, she felt certain that it was Mario, ready for 'round ninety-four' of their never-ending battle.

'Come in,' she called wearily.

A small, curly dark head appeared around the door.

'Mum said I'm not allowed to wake you,' chirped Tony. 'But you're awake already, aren't you?'

'I am now,' agreed Sandra with a yawn. She had been on duty in Casualty until midnight the night before. 'What can I do for you, Tony?'

He shut the door conspiratorially behind him, tiptoed across to her bed and sat gravely on the edge.

'I just want you to persuade Dad to leave me in Sydney when he goes to Italy for the summer opera season,' he said.

'Oh, is that all?' she groaned, burrowing back under the blankets. 'Are you sure you wouldn't like me to do something a bit easier for you? Like fly you to the moon or take you deep-sea diving?'

But irony was wasted on Tony.

'Come on, Sandra,' he pleaded. 'Willy Jessup's having his birthday party in August, and I'll miss it if we're in stupid old Italy. And besides, I'm in the school swimming team for the mid-winter indoor relay. I beat Matty Thomas in the heats, but they'll let him take my place if I'm not there. Oh, go on, Sandra. Ask Dad. Please—please!'

Sandra sat up and pushed her curls out

of her eyes with a sigh.

'Tony,' she said patiently, 'I've been asking your father for months to let you stay on in Sydney. He takes no notice. It's just a waste of time.'

Tony's lip jutted out.

'You just haven't asked him enough times,' he complained. 'He'll give in if you pester him enough. That's what I always do when I want something.'

'Don't I know it!' retorted Sandra. 'Look, Tony, I've tried everything to persuade your father to let you stay here, but I'm not beating my head against a brick wall any longer!'

A mutinous scowl came over his face, making him look astonishingly like his father.

'I'll run away if Dad tries to make me go to Italy!' he threatened.

'You naughty, silly boy!' cried Sandra reaching for him protectively. 'Don't you dare say such a thing, even as a joke!'

'I'm not joking,' he muttered, pulling away from her. 'And anyway, you haven't tried everything, Sandra. You should ask Richard to work on Dad.'

'What?' she exclaimed, utterly dumb-founded. 'Wherever did you get that idea?'

'I heard Mum say it to Mrs Jessup. She said, "Richard's one of the best, haemo ...haemo—you know, blood doctors—in Sydney. If anyone could convince Mario that Tony should stay here, Richard's the one." So why don't you ask Richard to try?'

Tony glared at her accusingly and Sandra felt the ground slipping dangerously away from under her feet.

'Tony,' she began pleadingly, 'you don't understand—'

'Yes, I do,' he cut in imperiously. 'You've had a stupid fight with Richard, so you don't care what happens to me any more. If you did, you'd ask him.'

Sandra stared at the child with an appalled expression. She knew that Tony was manipulating her outrageously, and yet at the same time she felt that there was a kernel of truth in his accusation. Sensing her indecision, he cast her a swift, pathetic look.

'Will you ask him, Sandra?' he said huskily. 'Please.'

She winced.

'Have you ever thought about being a door-to-door salesman when you grow up, Tony?' she demanded in a resigned voice.

'All right, I'll ask him.'

'Great!' he cried. Snatching the phone off her bedside table he set it on her lap.

'On Monday,' hedged Sandra.

'No, now!' insisted Tony. 'Go on, Sandy. Please, please. Phone him.'

She hesitated, fully aware that she was being conned. Tony locked his hands together and stared beseechingly at her. The wretched child! Somehow or other he always got his own way, yet this time she hardly cared whether he was getting spoilt. And he was right about one thing—she shouldn't let her own feelings interfere with Tony's welfare. Her fingers hesitated over the telephone receiver and an odd, fluttering sensation went through her at the thought of hearing Richard's voice. Anyway, with luck he wouldn't be home.

But the phone was answered immediately.

'Hello. Richard Daly speaking.'

'Richard?'

Her voice was barely more than a breathless squeak, but he recognised it at once.

'Sandra.'

It wasn't encouraging. His tone was

239

flat, wary, almost hostile. She paused despairingly, not knowing how to begin.

'What can I do for you?' he prompted sarcastically. 'I assume you haven't just rung up for a chat for old times' sake.'

'It's about Tony,' she said in a rush. 'Look, Richard, I know you don't want to speak to me any more than I do to you, but I think we ought to overcome our personal feelings for once. Mario is still insisting on taking Tony to Italy for the European summer and the poor kid's desperately unhappy about it. Couldn't you please, please speak to Mario about the medical arguments against it?'

'What? Begging, Sandra?' demanded Richard mockingly. 'I thought you had more pride!'

'When it comes to somebody I love, I have no pride whatsoever, Richard,' replied Sandra soberly.

There was a moment's silence. Then Richard's voice came down the line, cool and unemotional, but without the cutting undertone.

'What do you want me to do?'

'Could you come over and talk to Mario about it? Today might be a good time. He'll be home all day.'

Tony snatched the phone out of her hands.

'Hey, Richard?' he said eagerly. 'When you come, can you come by boat, not car? Then you can take me for a ride in the runabout after you finish talking to Dad!'

Sandra heard Richard's low growl of laughter on the other end of the line.

You little ratbag!' he reproved Tony. 'All right, I'll bring the boat. Tell Sandra I'll be there in half an hour.'

And, without so much as a word of farewell, the line went dead. Tony climbed on to the bed and bounced vigorously on the mattress, whooping and clapping.

'Stop that!' ordered Sandra in exasperation. 'All I need is for you to get another banged elbow today. Haven't you caused me enough trouble? Now go and get dressed while I soften up your dad for this meeting.'

Sandra was showered and dressed in five minutes. She deliberately resisted the impulse to put on a pretty frock or make-up for Richard's benefit and instead wore an old pair of blue jeans and a dark green shirt that she hated. Let him think she looked pale and hideous! What did she care? Anyway, it was Mario he was coming to meet, not her.

She found Mario in a lounge-chair on the terrace, conducting an imaginary orchestra with one hand and warbling under his breath between sips of strong black coffee. As the aria came to an end he looked up at her and frowned critically.

'*Mamma mia!*' he said. 'Where did you get those clothes? You look as if you're going to a grave-diggers' convention.'

Sandra ignored this piece of brotherly frankness and perched on the brick parapet overlooking the harbour.

'I want to ask you a favour,' she announced abruptly.

'Anything,' agreed Mario genially. 'Especially if it will bring the colour back to your cheeks.'

'Richard Daly's coming over here in half an hour. I want you to listen to what he says about Tony's medical treatment.'

Mario's fists clenched on the arms of his lounge-chair. His face darkened.

'Almost anything,' he amended.

'Mario, you promised!' flared Sandra.

'You're still in love with that bastard, aren't you?' he challenged.

'Whether I am or I'm not has nothing

to do with it!' cried Sandra impatiently. 'Richard Daly is a damned good doctor, Mario, and he's coming here as a doctor. Not as my lover or ex-lover or future lover! I'm finished with him, do you hear me? Finished!'

'You're sure?' demanded Mario suspiciously.

'Yes!'

'All right, I'll see him,' he agreed. 'But I make no promises about what I'll do.'

He picked up his coffee again, but this time he no longer sang. As she made her way back into the house Sandra felt her heartbeat quicken. I'm only doing this for Tony, she reminded herself, but she knew she was lying. However painful it might be, she could not wait to see Richard again herself.

CHAPTER TWELVE

When Sandra opened the door to Richard half an hour later her heart was thudding frantically in her chest. As always, the sight of him sent an uncomfortable thrill through her, but there was no sign of this in her face as she stood back unsmilingly to let him in.

'Have you been sick?' he asked bluntly, noting the shadows under her eyes and the look of strain around her mouth.

'No,' she replied curtly. 'It was good of you to come, Richard. Mario's waiting for you in the living-room, so please go straight in.'

Mario was standing with his back to the large marble fireplace and his legs planted apart aggressively. He looked up as Richard entered the room and something about that darting glance reminded Sandra of an all-in wrestler, sizing up his opponent. But Richard was not easily intimidated. His square jaw hardened and his mouth quirked into an amused smile.

'Hello, Mario,' he murmured, with an ironical lift of the eyebrows. 'Nice to see you again.'

He might have been Mario's best friend, strolling casually into the room with his hand outstretched. Except that Mario completely ignored the outstretched hand and shot Richard a look that was far more murderous than welcoming.

'Sit down,' he grunted.

With a careless shrug Richard sank into a deep leather armchair and stretched his long legs comfortably in front of him. But his gaze slewed away from Mario to Sandra, who was hovering by the door.

'I'll go and make some coffee,' she said hastily, turning away.

'Stop!' insisted Mario. 'I'll need you here to interpret for me.'

Sandra halted in her tracks and looked back reluctantly.

'I'd rather not,' she muttered.

'I believe you,' said Mario. 'And I'm sorry to ask it of you, *cara*. It can't be pleasant for you to be in the same room as this man who has seduced and abandoned you—'

Richard tensed forward in his chair like a lion about to spring.

'Just a damned minute!' he cut in. 'I'll have you know, Calvi, that Sandra left me, not the other way round.'

Sandra flushed scarlet, but held her anger and embarrassment in check.

'Can't we all behave like civilised adults about this?' she begged, looking reproachfully from one man to the other. 'After all, it's Tony we're here to talk about, not me.'

Mario shrugged expansively. 'All right. Talk,' he ordered.

With difficulty Richard dragged his gaze away from Sandra and looked down at his hands, which were now clasped tensely in front of him. Then, as if by an effort of will, he slowly relaxed. And when he spoke his voice had the pleasant, modulated tone that he used with inexperienced young registrars.

'Look, Mario,' he said, 'just forget that you hate my guts, OK? And try to remember that I'm an experienced haematologist. And, speaking in that capacity, I must tell you that you're endangering Tony's health by dragging him around the world so much. And perhaps even worse than his health. You may be risking his life.'

'Why?' demanded Mario aggressively. 'My son has had very few dangerous bleeding episodes. Very few. And they've always been successfully treated.'

Richard sighed impatiently.

'I'm glad to hear it,' he said. 'But haemostasis, or stopping the bleeding, is no longer the primary problem in treating haemophilia. Of course it's still vitally important, but the real challenge is to

246

provide haemophiliacs with the kind of care that will let them live as near normal a life as possible. Wouldn't you agree?'

'Maybe,' muttered Mario grudgingly.

'Well then,' continued Richard, warming to his theme, 'let me tell you that it's really only possible to do that when the patient is living in a stable environment, particularly when you're talking about a kid. If you have a good hospital close by with experienced staff, a bleeding episode is not a major problem. But if you're abroad in countries without good facilities, a minor accident can be potentially fatal. So far you've been lucky with Tony, but you can't count on your luck holding forever.'

'That's right!' chipped in Sandra. 'I've always felt, when I'm travelling with Tony, that there's a disaster just waiting to happen.'

'Don't say that!' muttered Mario uneasily, making a gesture with his fingers to avert the evil eye.

'Nevertheless, it's true,' insisted Richard, pressing home the advantage. 'I'm not sure how much you know about haemophilia, Mario, but you must understand the basics. Most haemophiliacs have a factor missing from their blood, which we call Factor VIII. Ever since the 1960s the widespread use of cryoprecipitates and blood concentrates has made it fairly easy to control bleeding and prevent crippling in most patients. But that only works if they get proper medical care and get it fast. What happens if Tony's in mid-air over the Pacific Ocean and the plane hits a pocket of turbulence? He falls and hits his knee and suffers bleeding into the joint. It may take several hours to get him to a hospital, and what happens to him in the meantime?'

Mario brushed that aside.

'We always strap him into his seat,' he protested.

Richard clenched his teeth and took a deep breath.

'All right,' he said. 'Forget about the dramatic incidents. How about the minor ones? Tony falls down the stairs in some foreign country and needs a blood transfusion. Have you thought about the diseases he could catch from it? Hepatitis B, malaria, HIV—AIDS. We screen for those things very carefully at the Blood Transfusion Service in Australia, but not all countries are so careful.'

Mario continued to look obstinately unconvinced.

'He's never had any trouble like that yet,' he retorted.

Richard clenched his fists tightly on his knees. His calm professional manner began to fray a little.

'Yet!' he snapped. 'That's the operative word. All right, leave aside all of that, Mario. I assume you want your son to have a normal life. A home, friends, training for a career, security. Don't you?'

'Of course I do!' snapped Mario. 'What do you think I am?'

'Well, all of that would be much easier to provide if you let him stay in one place. Once his illness is properly under control it will be a whole lot easier for him to get on with the rest of his life. I honestly think the best thing you could do for him as a father is to provide him with that kind of stability.'

'Oh, you do, do you?' shouted Mario. *'Cristo in croce,* you're a fine one to lecture me about stability and fatherhood! You, who have never been a father in your life, unless by accident! You, who entice my sister away and then send her home broken-hearted so that she lies in her room and cries every night!'

'Mario, stop it!' cried Sandra in horror. 'It's not true! I don't Richard, I don't!'

'You can't fool me, Sandra,' insisted Mario. 'And neither can you, il Dottor Daly. Ever since we first met you there's been nothing but trouble in this family. And let me tell you now, you are the last person whose advice I would accept about my son. Tony goes with me to Italy this summer and so do Lisa and Sandra. That's my final word on the matter!'

As Mario finished speaking there was a violent crash from outside the window. They all jumped, and Sandra, who was closest, ran to the window to investigate. On the terrace lay an overturned garden chair and beside it sat Tony with a scowl on his upturned face.

'Tony!' exclaimed Sandra in exasperation. 'Were you listening at the window?'

Then concern overwhelmed her annoyance as she saw that he was wincing with pain and clutching his knee.

'Oh, honey, have you hurt yourself?' she cried.

'You wouldn't care if I did!' shouted Tony, bursting into tears. 'None of you would, especially Dad. I hate you all, and

250

I'm running away!'

Scrambling to his feet, he dashed the tears away with the back of his hand, then broke into a stumbling run.

'Tony, come back!' called Sandra.

She drew her head hastily back inside the window and collided with Richard. He put his arms on her shoulders to steady her and, miserable as she was, she was conscious of a sudden feeling of safety.

'What's he done?' he demanded.

'Run off down the stairs again,' she retorted bitterly. 'No doubt he's going to lead us a great dance over the rocks, the little brat. Oh, and he says he's running away.'

Mario thrust his powerful shoulders out of the window and bellowed after his son.

'Antonio! *Torna qua! Subito!*'

Richard and Sandra exchanged looks.

'Come on!' ordered Richard, and they both shot out of the door.

But Tony had a substantial head start and was already well down the long staircase leading to the harbour. All the same, it was not until they reached the landing at the halfway point that the

251

first real fear clutched at Sandra with icy fingers.

'Oh, Richard!' she exclaimed. 'He's in our neighbour's dinghy. And it looks as though he's starting the outboard motor.'

'Tony!' roared Richard. 'Stop that at once!'

But Tony continued to tug desperately at the starter cord and, seconds later, the motor chugged into life. Up on the terrace Mario gave a cry of rage and dismay.

'You'll kill yourself, boy!' he stormed. 'Come back here or I'll stop your pocket money for the next year!'

'Don't worry, I'll catch him.' yelled Richard, and he went hurtling down the stairs at breakneck speed. 'I'll take the speedboat.'

Sandra followed suit and arrived sobbing and gasping on the jetty, just as Richard was about to cast off. She leapt nimbly aboard the bobbing craft and grabbed at the windscreen to steady herself. Then Richard dragged her into her seat as the boat went skimming across the water in a cloud of spray. Dimly her mind registered the emerald-green coldness of the water, the smell of salt in the air, the sense of speed and exhilaration as they bumped across the surface of the waves, but none of it touched her. All she could think of was the defiant little figure crouched over the tiller in the dinghy ahead of them. Tony was steering an erratic course and, as he heard the noise of pursuit, he glanced over his shoulder and then let the motor out to full throttle. The tiny dinghy changed direction yet again and leapt across the water like a bucking colt. Sandra let out a cry of fear.

'Richard! He'll run aground on Lizard Island if we don't catch him. It's just around the headland and I'll bet he's forgotten all about it.'

Richard swore under his breath and opened up the throttle to full power. As they rounded the headland the gap between the two boats began to close. But Sandra was right—Tony had forgotten all about Lizard Island. And, as he turned from glancing over his shoulder and saw its rocky shoreline looming ahead of him, he did what any nine-year-old would have done. He panicked. After one fruitless, fumbling attempt to turn off the motor he flung his arms up over his face and screamed as the dinghy smashed full tilt on the rocks.

Sandra's heart almost stopped as she saw his frail figure being flung forward against the bow of the craft. Yet somehow he managed to stagger to his feet and try to climb over the side of the boat. But as he did so another wave hit the dinghy beam-on and sent it surging down on top of him. There was a froth of white foam against the dark rocks and Tony vanished from sight.

'Oh, God! Oh, God!' breathed Sandra.

She wasn't even aware of climbing over the side of the speedboat, but the chill of the water sent a shock jolting through her. A mouthful of salty fluid went choking into her lungs and she came up spluttering, with her eyes full of wet hair. Rocks shifted under her feet and the tug of the waves threatened to sweep her on to the shore. Another figure appeared in the water beside her and she felt Richard's wet hand touch her arm.

'Don't look!' he warned, as he waded ahead of her towards the wrecked dinghy.

He thinks Tony's dead, she thought in horror. And when she saw Richard lift the limp body from the surging waves the scene around her began to disintegrate strangely into a mass of dancing grey spots. She gave a deep, moaning sigh.

'Don't faint on me, Sandra!' rapped out Richard. 'I need help with this kid.'

'He's...alive?'

'Barely. But he's got a chance.'

Blood began to flow in her veins again and her head cleared.

'What do we do?' she asked.

'Get him aboard and head for a hospital,' replied Richard curtly.

Once Tony was lying flat on the floor of the boat, wrapped in a space blanket, Richard used the radio to call for help.

'Pan-Pan. Pan-Pan,' he said urgently. 'This is Dr Richard Daly, aboard the *Jenny Mae* off Lizard Island. I've got a major medical emergency here—a nine-year-old haemophiliac child with a suspected ruptured spleen, needing an ambulance immediately to go from Clarence Cove jetty to the Nelson Hospital. He'll require emergency surgery on arrival at the Nelson, and that means a huge amount of blood. I want you to contact the central blood bank and get them to send a thousand units of Factor VIII under siren to the Nelson Hospital at once. Blood type O-positive. Have you got that? Over.'

There was a crackle of agreement on the other end of the line and Richard replaced the receiver with relief.

'OK, let's go,' he said, starting up the engine.

The trip to the hospital was a nightmare. Throughout the boat trip Tony remained waxy pale, his eyes closed and his face so expressionless that he seemed already dead. It would have been lunacy to try to carry him up the stairs at the Calvis' home, but fortunately Richard had foreseen that problem and the ambulance was waiting for them at the public jetty in Clarence Cove. As soon as they were inside the vehicle he inserted a drip in Tony's arm and shouted to the officer to hit the accelerator. The boy was in shock and certainly would not survive long without emergency treatment. After a high-speed dash, with the siren wailing dismally, they pulled into the emergency bay at the hospital. As soon as the ambulance officers lifted Tony out of the vehicle the casualty staff came racing to help him inside. Richard touched Sandra briefly on the shoulder.

'I'll have to go and get cleaned up,' he said. 'The casualty staff will do the usual emergency drill, but they'll need me in the lab as soon as they've taken blood samples. I'll have to do multiple assays and check that there's enough blood available. And they may want me in Theatre afterwards.'

All her anguish and hope and fear was in her eyes as she looked up at him. She clutched his shirt beseechingly and felt his warmth through the damp fabric.

'Save him, Richard,' she begged. 'Please, please save him.'

He disengaged her gently.

'We'll do all we can, love,' he muttered, avoiding her eyes. 'Now why don't you go and find his mum and dad? They'll probably need all the support they can get.'

But enquiry revealed that Mario and Lisa had not yet arrived at the hospital. A sympathetic but harrassed Cathy Wright was on duty in Casualty, and she took one look at Sandra and ordered her out.

'You're covered in sand and sea-water and you're on the verge of breaking down,' she summed up curtly. 'Now, have you got a spare uniform in your locker?'

'Yes,' gulped Sandra.

'Well, take a shower, get changed, and don't come back here until you've pulled yourself together.'

It was good advice. After her shower Sandra dragged on the spare uniform, spent five minutes weeping into a paper towel, then remembered that she was a nurse and not just an aunt. Blowing her nose and straightening her cap, she marched purposefully off towards Casualty.

She found Mario and Lisa sitting hand in hand on a blue-upholstered bench, looking lost and bewildered. In spite of their stylish clothes they had a haunting air of pathos, like a pair of refugees. Lisa was sobbing quietly into a handkerchief, and even Sandra's exuberant brother looked grey-faced and shocked. Sandra came to a halt in front of them.

'Can I get you some coffee?' she asked quietly.

Lisa jumped.

'Oh, Sandra!' she wailed. 'What's going on? Nobody will tell us anything, and they've got that awful curtain around Tony. And they took all kinds of strange equipment in. He's not dead, is he?'

'No, but he is very seriously ill,' said Sandra gravely.

'Will he die?' demanded Mario.

'I don't know,' admitted Sandra. A sob caught in her throat. 'But you must have faith,' she urged passionately. 'Richard's a splendid doctor and they're doing everything they possibly can. If anyone can save Tony, they will.'

'But what are they doing to him?' demanded Mario distractedly. 'What's wrong with the boy?'

Sandra hesitated, uncertain as to how much she should say.

'They think he has a ruptured spleen,' she said.

'What does that mean?' insisted Mario. 'What will happen to him?'

'He'll need massive blood transfusions and there's likely to be very heavy bleeding into the abdominal cavity. They'll have to give him heaps of Factor VIII and operate to remove the spleen.'

'But he might bleed to death anyway? Is that what you're saying?'

She paused, then let out her breath in a long sigh.

'Yes,' she admitted.

For the first time Mario noticed her

uniform. He touched the blue and white fabric like a man who could not believe that what he was seeing was real.

'And you?' he asked. 'Why are you dressed like this? Will you be taking part in this operation?'

Sandra shook her head.

'I'm not on duty,' she said. 'Besides, this hospital has a policy of not allowing staff to treat their own relatives. I can only do what you and Lisa must do: wait, and pray—'

Yet after a while Sandra could not bear the suspense any longer. Leaving Mario and Lisa to their thoughts, she walked distractedly across to the haematology building and crept into the lab. Richard was already at work, wearing a lab coat and gloves and peering down at a machine in front of him.

'What are you doing?' she asked miserably.

A swift look of sympathy passed between them.

'Checking his clotting factors,' replied Richard. 'I spin the blood to get plasma, mix it with calcium chloride, a lipid and a plasma known to be deficient, and then check it against a normal control.'

260

'And how is it?' she asked with a tremor in her voice.

'Not too good,' he replied heavily.

She stared imploringly at him. She had forgotten all about their quarrel. At this moment the only thing that seemed to matter was the fact that she would trust Richard with her life. Or Tony's life.

'Richard,' she said, biting back tears, 'if the surgeon will let you into Theatre while they operate, will you please be there? I just don't want to feel that Tony will be all alone, if anything happens...'

'Of course, I will, darling,' he said gently.

But Sandra was so upset that she did not even notice what he had called her.

It was nearly two hours later when Richard came walking down the corridor to the waiting area near the operating theatre, accompanied by the surgeon Chris Warwick. Richard's face was shadowed with fatigue and there were lines of anxiety etched around his mouth. Sandra's heart did a slow, plummeting dive as the two men came to a halt in front of Mario, and Lisa.

'Mr and Mrs Calvi?' said the surgeon. 'We've news about your son.'

CHAPTER THIRTEEN

They all held their breath as the surgeon's face creased into a tired smile.

'Good news,' he added reassuringly. 'We're not out of the woods yet, but Tony's holding his own better than I expected. The spleen was damaged and we had to remove it, but the boy's come through the operation well. We're going to put him into the intensive care unit now and, if all goes well, within two or three days he should be out of danger.'

Mario swayed on his feet.

'Thank God,' he muttered. 'And thank you, Mr Warwick.'

'It's really Dr Daly you should be thanking,' replied Chris. 'He's got the haematology section here organised like clockwork. Without him we'd have had a much tougher job supplying the blood that Tony needed.'

Mario turned to Richard with an anguished look on his face.

'There are no words for what I owe

262

you, Dr Daly,' he murmured humbly. 'No words. No words.'

He bit his lip and couldn't go on. Suddenly, with a roar of relief, he enfolded Richard in a mighty bear-hug, lifted him clean off the floor and thumped him violently on the back.

'May God bless you!' he said through his teeth.

Then it was Lisa's turn to hug Richard and smile radiantly at him through her tears. And, last of all, Sandra found herself confronting him. Suddenly the onlookers and the busy hospital corridor seemed to spin away, leaving the two of them in a void. Sandra was dimly conscious of the smell of antiseptic, a fluorescent light that was buzzing weirdly overhead, a gritty particle of sand that had lodged in one of her shoes. But the only thing that held her attention was the tall, golden-haired man who stood staring down at her so piercingly. Her heart beat a wild tattoo as she raised her blue eyes to his. In that moment she knew that she loved him as deeply as ever.

'Oh, Richard,' she breathed.

He took a step towards her, caught her in his arms and crushed her against him, heedless of the onlookers. His lips touched her hair and he breathed deeply, inhaling her warm feminine scent.

'Sandra, can't we stop this stupid quarrel we've been having?' he demanded. 'You must realise by now what a load of rubbish that was about Felicity Hamilton! I only had lunch with them because her mother's such a brilliant fund-raiser, but I certainly didn't sleep with Felicity and I never will. For the simple reason that I'm in love with another woman. You.'

Sandra's breath caught in her throat and she gazed at him despairingly, longing for it to be true and yet fearing that it wasn't. With a cry of exasperation he cupped her face in his hands and stared down at her with his blazing, lion's eyes.

'I love you, you idiot!' he exclaimed. 'Don't you understand? I love you! I don't want another woman—ever.'

Then his mouth came down on hers and he kissed her with all the warmth of a passionate nature held too long in check. Blissfully she settled into his arms and kissed him back. There was a faint rasping noise as Chris Warwick cleared his throat. Scarlet with embarrassment, Sandra came hurtling back to earth.

'Sorry!' she muttered, then clapped a hand over her mouth to stifle a giggle.

'Perhaps you might like to continue this discussion somewhere a little more private?' suggested Chris with a lift of the eyebrows.

'Good idea,' agreed Richard, not in the least taken aback. 'Come on, Sandra.'

A couple of hours later they were in the living-room of Richard's house, looking out over the darkening harbour. On the north shore the lights twinkled like Christmas decorations, and when Richard opened the French doors to bring in more wood a chill breeze nipped in at his heels. But inside the house it was warm and welcoming. Orange flames crackled in the hearth, a tall lamp with a satin fringe cast a soft glow of light across the Persian carpet and the sound of haunting piano music rippled forth from the CD player. Sandra relaxed against the gold velvet sofa cushions, enjoying the delicious sensation of returning home. Yet in spite of her joy she felt a certain sense of apprehension. Coming here like this, it was easy to feel that nothing had changed between her and Richard. And yet deep down she knew that things would have to change if their love was to have any future. And somehow she must make Richard see that too. There was a sudden hiss of sparks as he threw a fresh log on the fire, then he came and sat beside her.

'What are you thinking?' he asked, drawing one of her curls through his fingers so that it uncoiled and then snapped back like a spring.

She smiled warily and took a sip of her sherry, enjoying its clean, nutty flavour on her palate.

'That it feels like coming home, being back here,' she murmured. 'As if nothing has changed between us.'

'That's good,' he said, taking her sherry ruthlessly from her hand and setting it down on an inlaid occasional table. Drawing her tightly into his arms, he snuggled his head into her thick blonde curls. 'You wouldn't believe how much I missed you,' he said throatily. 'I went around the house, collecting up everything that could possibly remind me of you and dumping it in a big green bin-bag. I was going to put it all in one of those charity bins and I thought that would rid me of you forever. But when it came to the point I couldn't bear to part with any of it. Can

266

you imagine anything more ridiculous than a thirty-nine-year-old man, clutching a bag full of old magazines and hairspray, unable to let go of it?'

'No,' admitted Sandra wryly. 'Unless it's a woman of twenty-six who thinks every traffic warden and bus driver and shop assistant with gold hair is the one man she's hoping and fearing to meet.'

'Were you really hoping to meet me?' he asked.

'Every minute,' she said ruefully. 'Every single rotten minute.'

He gave a low groan and squeezed her so tightly that she gasped.

'Then why did you leave me, you heartless wench?' he demanded.

'What a question' she protested. 'I left because I thought you were sleeping with Felicity Hamilton, of course.'

Richard ran his fingers through his hair and heaved an exasperated sigh.

'But how could you believe such rubbish?' he demanded. 'You were stupid ever to imagine that it could be true, Sandra.'

'Was I?' she said unsteadily.

Scrambling to her feet, she prowled across to the fireplace and stood with one arm on the mantelpiece, staring at him appraisingly. Somehow she felt the need to put distance between them, as if her judgement would not work clearly while she was close to his hypnotic touch and warmth and smell.

'What's that supposed to mean?' asked Richard sharply.

Sandra sighed.

'Just this,' she retorted. 'You say I was stupid to believe that you'd sleep with Felicity. But was I really so stupid? After all, from the first time I met you, you made it clear that you were a playboy, that you'd had heaps of affairs and that commitment was a dirty word to you. Why was I being stupid to think that you might be unfaithful to me?'

'Because it was different with you!' he protested. 'You weren't like the others. There was something really special between us.'

'Was there?' she retorted sceptically.

'Yes!' he said, rising from the sofa and taking a step towards her. 'And there still is.'

'Don't come any closer,' she warned, gazing at him warily.

'Why not?' demanded Richard.

'Because I know you!' exclaimed Sandra

bitterly. 'You'll start kissing me and touching me, and before long we'll be ripping our clothes off and making love on the floor. But that's not what I want!'

'Isn't it?' murmured Richard throatily, looking at her through narrowed eyes.

'No,' she said. 'At least, not by itself. I've been doing a lot of thinking since I left you, Richard, and I've come to one conclusion: that I should never have made love with you in the first place.'

'Thanks,' he sneered. 'Strange, isn't it? I was always under the impression that you enjoyed our lovemaking. That all those little sighs and moans meant that you were getting pleasure from it, not that you were secretly wishing you could go and scrub the cooker. Shows how wrong you can be, doesn't it?'

'Oh, don't be so ridiculous!' she snapped. 'Of course I enjoyed it, but that's not the point! There are probably scores of other men who could give me just as much pleasure as you did. What I'm—'

'Don't bet on it!' muttered Richard sourly.

Sandra ignored the interruption and went doggedly on.

'What I'm trying to say is that sex is not

only a matter of pleasure to me,' she said earnestly. 'It's also tied up with some of the deepest feelings I have. Feelings about love and marriage and commitment. And I should never have tried to have one without the other, because it was just ripping me in half. Oh, I know women aren't supposed to say that these days, are they? It's not modern or sophisticated or trendy, but I'll tell you something, Richard. Women's feelings aren't modern or sophisticated or trendy either. They're as old and primitive as time itself. Or at least mine are.'

He was watching her with a crooked smile playing around the corners of his mouth. Now he stretched out his arms and took a step towards her.

'Come here,' he urged.

'No,' she said in a tormented voice. 'Not until we get this sorted out. I don't want to go back to where we were before. Living with you and worrying all the time about whether you're making love to somebody else. Being on bad terms with my family because they think you're exploiting me. Having to pretend at work that I live somewhere else. It's not enough for me, Richard.'

'It's not enough for me either, Sandra,' he retorted abruptly. 'You're not the only one who's been thinking while we were apart.'

'W-what do you mean?' she faltered.

'Simply that I took a good, hard look at myself and didn't much like what I saw. I've been running scared for years, having meaningless affairs, trying to avoid any real commitment. Until I met you. I won't pretend that I changed overnight, but a funny thing happens when you spend a lot of time with one person. You start to see things through her eyes.' He was silent, staring into the fire.

'And so?' urged Sandra.

'And so, bit by bit, I began to consider the things that you thought were important. like having a family whom you could count on and who could count on you. Making a public commitment and honouring it. It seemed like a pretty satisfying lifestyle to have. The only trouble was that I didn't think I could ever live up to it. Or not at first.'

'And now?' she prompted huskily.

Richard crumpled a piece of newspaper and threw it into the heart of the fire,

271

where it burst instantly into flame.

'And now I think it's time I stopped collecting scalps and found a few new hobbies,' he said. 'Like coming home early in the evenings, doing the garden, taking my wife to hospital balls—'

'Did you say "wife"?' asked Sandra in a choking voice.

'Mm,' he agreed, carefully avoiding her gaze.

'Well?' she prompted.

His tawny eyes met hers and they were suddenly alight with mischief. But all he did by way of reply was to lounge across to the davenport desk that stood in a corner of the room and take a flexible tape-measure out of one of its drawers. Strolling back to the fireplace, he took Sandra's left hand in his and gravely measured her ring finger.

'Six centimetres exactly,' he murmured. 'Sandra, this is purely a hypothetical question, but, just as a matter of interest, tell me this. If I asked you to marry me, what would you say?'

An incredulous joy dawned in her face.

'Oh, Richard!' she cried, flinging herself into his arms and hugging him. 'I'd say yes, of course!'

He kissed her with a deep, lingering urgency that made her heart beat frantically and her breath come in shallow gulps. When at last they drew apart she gazed up at him with misty eyes.

'Well, go on,' she urged. 'Aren't you going to ask me to marry you?'

He grinned wickedly.

'Oh, no, not right now,' he said. 'I did warn you that it was a purely hypothetical question.'

Two weeks later Sandra was kneeling on the floor of her room, sealing some cartons with masking tape, when her brother Mario knocked at the half-open door.

'Lisa sent me to ask you two things,' he announced. 'First of all, did you remember to invite Richard to dinner tonight?'

'Yes,' said Sandra, biting off a length of tape. 'Next question?'

'Lisa and I are going to fetch Tony from the hospital in an hour or so. Do you want to come with us?'

'No, thanks, Mario,' she replied. 'I think he'd probably rather be alone with you. Besides, I'm busy packing.'

Mario's eyebrows drew together in a sudden frown. He sat down heavily on

Sandra's bed and glared down at the boxes.

'What for?' he demanded bluntly.

Sandra hid a smile.

'Because I'm likely to be moving back to Richard's place very soon,' she replied.

'Look,' began Mario with a volcanic scowl on his face, 'I won't deny that he's a brilliant doctor and he saved my son's life. But if he thinks—'

She cut in swiftly, 'Would it make you feel any better if I told you that Richard and I will be getting married later this year?'

His scowl evaporated to be replaced by a wide grin of delight. *'Bene, bene,'* he muttered approvingly. 'So Richard finally had the decency to propose to you, did he?'

'No,' said Sandra tranquilly and a mischievous smile spread over her face. 'But he will.'

The dinner that night was one of the most joyful family occasions Sandra had ever known. Tony was still weak and pale from his ordeal, but he was obviously happy to be home. Lisa had cooked a superb meal of lasagne, followed by chicken *cacciatora*, salad and lemon gelato. And, best of all,

Mario and Richard were treating each other like old friends. By the time they reached the stage of drinking fragrant espresso coffee they were chatting about everything under the sun from Mario's European concert plans to Richard's fund-raising efforts.

'Well, I have to admit one thing,' said Mario expansively, helping himself to a hazelnut wafer, 'you were right about Tony's illness, Richard, and I was wrong. The boy will be much better off living in the one place, much as it hurts me to think of it. But from now on, when I go on tour, Lisa and Tony will stay here.'

Richard reached across the table and shook hands with him.

'Good for you,' he said warmly. 'You're doing the right thing, I'm sure of it.'

Mario sighed.

'I know,' he agreed heavily. 'But it will break my heart to part from them. And it's a pity about the trip in July. My mother's over seventy and Lisa's parents aren't getting any younger. They all look forward to seeing the boy each summer.'

Sandra cleared her throat.

'Richard,' she said hesitantly, 'you did say something once about going to Italy with me just for a couple of weeks. Do you think if Tony had his own private haematologist and nurse with him that he could risk the trip for once?'

This brought a buzz of excitement and speculation. Lisa had to bring out airline schedules, Richard checked his diary for dates, Tony demanded to be home in time for Willy Jessup's birthday and Mario opened a bottle of the Orvieto *abboccato* wine so that Richard could see for himself what delights awaited him in Italy. When the uproar died down Sandra suddenly let out a groan of disappointment.

'But we'd have to leave on the first of July,' she pointed out. 'And your gala fund-raising dinner for the new coagulometer is on the fifth, isn't it, Richard?'

Richard grimaced.

'It's not on at all now, I'm afraid,' he said curtly. 'Mrs Hamilton has pulled out of organising it.'

'What? But why?' demanded Sandra.

He gave an embarrassed shrug.

'Well, it seems that when I kissed you in the corridor after Tony's operation word got around the hospital rather fast,' he explained. 'Felicity Hamilton rang me up to demand an explanation and I told her flatly that I was in love with you. She took offence and not long after Ms Hamilton senior was on the phone telling me haughtily that they wanted nothing further to do with me.'

Mario's black brows drew together ominously.

'What did you do to this...this Felicity?' he demanded.

Richard winced.

'Had lunch with her a couple of times and picked her brains about fashion parades and other ways of raising money,' he said.

'Hm,' snorted Mario. 'And this coagulometer? What is it?'

It was Sandra who replied.

'It's a piece of equipment that Richard wants to buy for the haematology section,' she replied. 'It's used for doing factor assays and diagnosing problems like haemophilia. But it costs about forty thousand dollars, and at the moment we're at least ten thousand dollars short. Mrs Hamilton was going to organise a gala charity dinner to raise funds for it.'

Mario slammed his hand down on, the table.

'Tch!' he said contemptuously. 'I spit on

her dinner! I have a much better idea for raising this money you need. I will give you a concert at the opera house and donate all the proceeds to the hospital. It will be my way of thanking you both.'

On a cold, starry evening three weeks later Sandra and Richard climbed the stairs of the opera house, arm in arm, and went into one of the large theatres. Mario had arranged for them to have a box with a superb view of the stage and, as the usher showed them the way, Sandra was thrilled to see that nearly every one of the seats in the auditorium was filled. A low hum of conversation rose from the assembled audience and several heads turned admiringly to watch them as they passed. Although Sandra was not aware of it they made a strikingly handsome couple. Richard's tall, lean frame was set off to perfection by the black dinner suit and his burnished hair gleamed brightly. Sandra herself floated like a graceful ballerina in a pale blue evening dress with a low-cut, flounced neck and sleeves of transparent spotted tulle. As they took their seats she saw Lisa and Tony in the box opposite them. Tony still looked rather pale, but he gave her a cheeky wave.

When the house lights went down Sandra felt the almost mystic sense of excitement that the theatre never failed to wake in her. She was not a performer like her brother, but she could not help longing to be there on the stage at the heart of it all. What a feeling it must be to know that the silent, expectant audience was yours to command! With parted lips, she leaned forward eagerly in the half darkess. Richard smiled and squeezed her hand. The warm touch of his fingers sent a current of happiness tingling through her. This is a perfect night, she thought rapturously. If I live to be a hundred, there will never be another night quite like this.

Then the curtains drew back and the spotlight scttlcd on the centre of the stage. A short, stocky figure in evening dress strode confidently into that circle of fight and gave the warm smile for which Mario Calvi was famous. There was a spontaneous burst of applause from the audience, but Mario held up both hands for silence.

'Ladies and gentlemen,' he said as the sound died away, 'you all know why we're here tonight. Recently my only son Tony nearly died after a boating accident on the harbour. But, as you can see, he is alive and well and with us at this moment—'

The spotlight cut away to the box where Tony and Lisa were sitting. Showing off outrageously, Tony rose to his feet and bowed to the audience with a wide, delighted grin.

'But the only reason Tony is still with us,' continued Mario, 'is the skill and dedication of the doctors and nurses at the Nelson Private Hospital. The debt I owe these wonderful people can never be fully repaid, but I do want to say thank you to them. So I've spoken to my old friends Giuseppe Ponti and Orlando Toscani—' again the spotlight moved '—and we've decided to give this benefit concert. All proceeds from the concert will go to the Nelson Hospital to buy medical equipment. And now, to begin tonight's entertainment, I'd like to sing the aria Nessun dorma!'

Sandra felt an instant of irrational regret that she and Richard had not enjoyed a brief moment in the spotlight too, then the orchestra began to play and all thoughts were swept away on a glorious tide of music. All three tenors performed brilliantly that night, but Mario Calvi sang like a man inspired. As the last notes died away, just before the interval, Sandra took a deep, shaky breath and looked at Richard.

'Wasn't he magnificent?' she breathed. 'No wonder they call him the one and only Mario Calvi.'

Richard looked amused.

'Yes, he was,' he admitted. 'Still, if you ask me, he's not half so magnificent as the one and only Sandra Calvi.'

She wrinkled her nose at him.

'Thanks,' she said affectionately. 'But I really don't think you're appreciating this concert properly, Richard.'

He smiled enigmatically.

'Oh, yes, I am,' he retorted. 'And I have a feeling I'm going to appreciate it even more before the end of the evening.'

She looked baffled and then shrugged. 'Come on,' she said. 'If we don't go downstairs now, we won't get a drink.'

Richard laid a restraining hand on her arm.

'Don't worry,' he told her. 'I'm having something sent up.'

A moment later there was a tap at the door and a black-coated usher came in with a silver tray containing a bottle of French champagne and two long-stemmed crystal glasses. But there were two other items on the tray which made Sandra's heart give a violent lurch. One was a rather large jewellery case covered in gold velvet. The other was a far smaller case, just the right size to hold a ring.

'Thank you,' said Richard, tipping the usher. 'Just leave the tray on the stool, will you?'

As the man closed the door behind him, Richard smiled lazily at Sandra, his tawny eyes gleaming.

'Well,' he murmured throatily, 'would you like the champagne before or after?'

'A—after what?' she faltered.

'After I ask you a rather important question,' replied Richard.

His gaze held hers for a moment, then he opened the larger of the two boxes to reveal a magnificent diamond necklace. Sandra caught her breath as she saw the light winking and dancing from that cascade of gems.

'Oh, Richard,' she breathed. 'Is that really a present for me?'

He drew it out of its box and fastened it around her neck, before dropping a warm kiss on her bare shoulder.

'Yes,' he said. 'And I'd like you to

keep it, whatever your answer is to my question.'

She bit her lip and then smiled tremulously at him.

'What's the question?' she murmured huskily.

Slowly he opened the second box and picked up the gold and diamond ring that lay inside.

'Will you be my wife?' he asked.

For one joyful instant time seemed to stand still. Then happy tears sprang to Sandra's eyes.

'Yes!' she cried. 'Oh, yes, Richard!'

He slid the ring silently down her finger, then kissed her briefly on the lips.

'I love you, Sandra,' he said simply. 'Now, shall we open the champagne?'

The rest of the concert passed in a rapturous daze for Sandra, but it wasn't quite the end of the surprises. For when Mario came on stage to thunderous applause for his final encore the house lights came on for a moment and he looked up at Richard's and Sandra's box. Richard rose lazily to his feet and held up his thumb and forefinger in a triumphant circle. The lights dimmed again and the spotlight returned to Mario.

'Ladies and gentlemen,' he said in vibrant tones, 'I've left the biggest acknowledgment of all till last. The people I have to thank most for saving my son's life are my sister Sandra Calvi and Dr Richard Daly. They have just become engaged tonight, and this final aria is specially for them. Sandra and Richard, would you please come down on stage?'

To her amazement Sandra found that the spotlight suddenly swung round to fix her in its glare. For a moment she stood paralysed in its brightness, then an usher came to lead them down to the backstage area. The light followed them as they moved and a storm of clapping rose about them. Once they reached the wings Sandra had time to catch her breath and stare disbelievingly up at Richard.

'Did you arrange this?' she asked.

'Yes,' he admitted, pulling her arm through his. 'You told me once that your secret fantasy was to be in the spotlight just once. And I wanted this to be a night you'd never forget.'

As he pulled her on to the stage Sandra felt a wild surge of excitement crest through her. Mario came to meet them, hugged them both warmly and shook Richard vigorously by the hand. When the applause died down he looked out at the audience.

'This time,' he said in a hushed voice, 'I want Sandra and Richard to have the limelight. They deserve it. Sandra and Richard, may God bless you both.'

An eerie silence followed as Mario moved out of the spotlight and away to a darkened corner of the stage. For a long, long moment Sandra stood in the circle of light, with Richard's arms clasped warmly around her, aware that all eyes were upon them and that everyone wished them well. Then out of the darkness came Mario's incredible voice. All the passion and heartbreak of love were poured into that thrilling aria and, as it came to a close, the audience remained silent and spellbound. Until Richard, like the prince in the fairytale, broke the spell by turning Sandra's face up to his and kissing her warmly on the lips. Then a low ground swell of sound began to hum through the theatre and people rose to their feet and clapped and clapped until their palms were sore. Soon the uproar filled the entire theatre. But, in the centre of the spotlight the man and the woman stayed locked in each other's arms, oblivious to everything but the power of love.

The publishers hope that this book has given you enjoyable reading. Large Print Books are especially designed to be as easy to see and hold as possible. If you wish a complete list of our books, please ask at your local library or write directly to: Dales Large Print Books, Long Preston, North Yorkshire, BD23 4ND, England.